The Peculiar Children Of Bus 13

Book 1: The New Girl

Tory C Anderson

Cover art: Sarah Hunt

Published by Oryander Publishing
PO Box 445 Levan UT 84639

Library of Congress Control Number: 2017917699

ISBN-10: 1979733856
ISBN-13: 978-1979733854

DEDICATION

To the children of the very real Bus 13. You changed my life.

Acknowledgments

I would like to thank my wife, Barbara, for supporting the dreams of a writer. Glory, your feedback during the writing process is invaluable. Eva Call is one fantastic copy editor. Sarah Hunt, the magic you work on my covers is, well, magical.

CONTENTS

1   Who Are You?   1

2   Bric-a-Brac and SpongeBob
    SquarePants   6

3   Felicia's Feline Muffins   12

4   The Pipes of Jimmy Backman   17

5   Don't Make Me Turn on the Radio   24

6   The Historic Arrival of Veronica Dover   31

7   Fog On a Clear Day   40

8   Wolves   48

9   Here Doggy, Doggy   55

10 Of Heroes and Cowards   64

11 I Will Scream   71

12 Oh, Dear   78

13 The Magic of Rosalie   87

14 Arrival   94

15 A Little Prank   105

16 Out-tricking a Trickster   112

17 Keep Its Secrets   117

18   Oranges and Fish and Bumps   123
      and Bruises

19   Fitting In, Or Not   133

20   Behold the Power   143

21   Like the Wind   154

22   Bad Magic   163

23   Do I Care?   170

24   Not Particularly Peculiar   179

CHAPTER 1 – WHO ARE YOU?

It was dark when Cali arrived at the bus stop. She could still see remnants of the Milky Way being soaked up by the graying eastern horizon. She couldn't get over the number of stars in the sky. In Salt Lake City, where she had lived until just a few days ago, there were so few stars she never even bothered to look up.

It was only her third morning living in 'the fields.' That's what the locals of Warburton called it when you lived in the farmlands west of town. Her little brick house was on a country lane surrounded by farmers' fields. She could see the lights of other lonely homes scattered across the fields. Warburton was a low patch of twinkling lights three miles east of where she stood.

Cali glanced over her shoulder, up the driveway, to her house. The only light she saw was the yard light shining through the limbs of the blue spruce. Had her parents gone back to bed?

"Figures," she mumbled. This was her first day at a new school and they were sending her alone. They weren't bad parents; Cali was just a capable girl, and they knew it.

The bus will pick you up at the end of the driveway, her mother had said.

Cali looked up the road for headlights. Nothing. She considered how embarrassed she would be if she stood here until the sun rose and the bus never came. The kids at her new school would find out somehow. She would be branded a loser from day one. She was a loner, not a loser. The kids would figure that out. It would just be uncomfortable while they did.

Cali heard the bus before she saw it—a rumble and a hiss of brakes. She jumped back as headlights blinded and disconcerted her. There was half a mile of road to the nearest intersection. She had a clear view. Where had it come from so suddenly? Her knees wobbled a little as she walked around the front of the bus to the door. It opened with a hiss and a clunk as she approached.

Cali looked up the steps expecting to see the bus driver. She saw nothing but darkness. Goosebumps ran up her arms. It was like looking into the opening of a cave at night. The fear left as she felt something passing out of the bus through the open door. It was like the bus was exhaling except that there was no air movement. It enticed her like a sweet smell, a savory taste, and a soft touch all at once. It was . . . *magical*. The word came suddenly, but gently.

"Who *are* you?" The voice floated out of the darkness. It was a man's voice, but it had some extra quality that made it slightly more than a man's voice—it was a man's voice with sparkles.

"Is . . . isn't this my bus?"

"That depends on who you are."

"I'm Cali, Cali McAllister."

"Cali MaCali," the voice said, bemused. "I like it. Did your parents do that on purpose?"

"Yes, um, no—I don't know," Cali said. Feeling restless she shifted her weight from one foot to the other. "So is this my bus?"

"That depends on who you are."

Ah, there he is, Cali thought. Out of the blackness she saw the faintest outline of his silhouette against the window behind him.

"I just told you," Cali said, impatiently. "My mom called Friday and made sure I qualified to ride the bus."

"You told me what your name is, not who you are."

If this were an ordinary school bus Cali would have told the driver to forget it. She didn't need this kind of game so early in the morning. Her mom could take her to school. This bus was not ordinary. *Magic* flowed out of the bus enticing her, like a moth to light. Some people want to be accepted to Harvard. Others dream of Julliard. From the moment the bus doors opened, Cali's greatest desire was to get on. The bus driver was the Sphinx with a riddle. Everything depended on her answer.

Cali's mind spun like car tires stuck in the snow—*Who am I? Who am I?* She struggled to come up with something important. She was an only child. Her parents were lawyers. She got mainly Bs in school. She was a loner so quiet that no one hardly ever noticed her. She had no close friends. *Is that who I am?*

Cali looked up at the bus driver who appeared to be willing to wait all day for her answer. Feeling a pang of despair she said, "I don't know."

Cali waited. The bus driver thought. The diesel engine at the rear of the bus idled.

Finally he spoke. "Promising," he said. "Most promising."

Cali felt sweet relief and a thrill of hope.

"But still questionable."

Her hope faltered.

"It will have to be your decision, but I give you this warning: if you ride this bus you will most likely find out who you are. If you think you can handle that truth, then enter."

Cali took a deep breath of joy tinged with fear. She was being given a gift. But a question tugged at her tongue. "What happens if I can't handle it?"

The bus driver answered slowly, but clearly. "The truth sets some people free; others, it crushes."

Deep inside an alarm rang. Instinct told her to walk away. The magic, it called to her. A neglected streak of stubbornness kicked in— she climbed the first step.

The moment her foot touched the step the magical spell began dissolving. It was as if she was awaking from a dream. She reached the third step and the magic was gone. She tripped over the top step and fell forward knocking the garbage can over.

"That last step's a doozy," the bus driver said. "You aren't the first one who's done that."

Embarrassed, Cali struggled to her feet and looked into the face of one of the most ordinary-looking bus drivers she had ever seen. He was a middle-aged man with a slightly large nose wearing square glasses. A black conductor's cap sat on his head. He was tinted orange by the dashboard lights.

What a disappointment—he was just another bus driver. This was just another bus. She felt so foolish that she couldn't even bring herself to say hello.

The driver didn't seem to notice. "You can sit anywhere you like. The kids on this bus are all friendly, although a bit curious." He turned back to the front adding, "Nobody's bit anybody . . . yet, anyway." He laughed nervously.

He's joking, of course, Cali thought. She wasn't amused.

Cali looked up the aisle into the darkness. Goosebumps ran up her arms a second time. It was pitch black and dead quiet. She couldn't see anyone, but she sensed eyes watching.

Silly! Silly! Silly! She mumbled, patting the top of each seat for courage as she passed. At the fourth seat something touched her hand. She heard the distinct sound of sniffing—the kind a dog makes when it's found something interesting. Cali squealed and lurched away falling into an empty seat across the aisle. A head rose, framed by the window behind it.

"You had Fruit Loops for breakfast," said a thin, low voice.

It was just a girl. Cali remembered to breathe. She could see the silhouette of frizzy hair. Was that a bow on the side? Blue eyes looked her way. That was wrong. She shouldn't be able to see eyes in the dark—unless they were glowing. And they *were* glowing, softly like the afterglow of a lightbulb that's just been turned off.

"I used to like Fruit Loops," said the girl, a little sadly, then sunk back down into the shadows of her seat. Her eyes blinked once, but remained visible.

"Shelley?" the driver called. "You smelling the new girl? I told you it's not nice to smell the new kids."

The eyes blinked. Cali pulled herself to her feet and hurried farther back into the bus. Finding what she hoped was an empty seat she sat down right next to the aisle.

She reached her hand toward her window. "Hello?" she said in a timid voice. She was relieved to find she was the only one in this seat.

"Hello," said two voices across the aisle.

Cali stifled another squeal. The tops of two heads were silhouetted against the window. There was a *click* as a clasp was unlatched. She watched as the top of what looked like a lunch box opened. Soft, green light flowed out of the box illuminating two boys. Identical bangs touched identical glasses that framed identical eyes.

"Hello. Let me introduce myself," the one nearest the aisle said. "I'm Marcus."

"And I'm Marty." The other boy leaned forward and flashed Cali a smile. "Could we offer you an energy drink this morning?" Marty pulled a test tube out of the lunch box. The liquid in it reminded her of the inside of a glow stick.

Showing perfect teamwork Marcus pulled out a glass bottle with a stopper on top. It made a squelching sound and then a *pop* as he pulled it off. Carefully he poured a few drops of the contents into the test tube. The liquid in the test tube appeared to bubble for a half-second before emitting a puff of smoke through the opening.

Marty offered the test tube to Cali. "All natural," he said.

"And no caffeine," added Marcus.

"Don't worry, the test tube is clean," said Marty. "Marcus washed the set last night."

"Me? No, it was your turn."

"Was not!" Marty turned quickly. The test tube slipped from his fingers and dropped to the floor. Glass shattered, liquid splashed, and the smell of overripe fruit reached Cali's nose.

"Excuse me," Cali mumbled. She leapt to her feet and hurried toward the front of the bus. Too late she remembered the girl with the eyes. She leaned away from her as she passed. Off balance, Cali glanced off the seat opposite which set off a chain reaction. She bumped back and forth off the other seats until she reached the front. She wanted off the bus.

Chapter 2 – Bric-a-Brac and SpongeBob SquarePants

"I would like to get off this bus, please," Cali said.

The bus driver jerked in his seat and gave a squeal. Cali squealed again.

"What are you doing?" he said, putting his hand over his heart. "You think we have time for me to go home to change my pants? You scared me."

Catching her breath, and trying to control the trembling in her voice, Cali said again, "I've decided that I don't want to ride this bus."

A hand grabbed her arm from behind. "Excuse me."

This time Cali didn't bother with a squeal—she went straight to tears.

"Why don't you take that seat right there, Cali" said the driver, "and give me a moment." Speaking over his shoulder he said to Marty, "Look what you did."

"We've just been trying to be friendly, but, *Marcus*," he spoke loudly, "made me drop the tube."

"*Did not*," a voice yelled back.

"Oh, gee whiz," said the driver. "Is this gonna stink like last time? If it does, you two are going to have to fumigate the bus yourselves."

"No, it was only our morning special."

"Oh, that stuff's pretty good," said the driver, licking his lips.

"We think so."

"Well, you know where the broom is. Here's the paper towels and wipes," the driver said passing them over his shoulder.

Marty took the items and grunted as he pulled a broom from between the seats and the windows on the driver's side.

"I don't want anything crunching or glowing back there when you get off," the driver said.

"Don't worry, Mr. Fennelmyer." Marty disappeared up the aisle.

While Mr. Fennelmyer was taking care of business with Marty Cali's feelings of panic passed. She became aware of how silly her crying sounded—like the squeaking wheel on her little cousin's toy wagon.

Why am I crying, anyway? she asked herself. *Sure, a bus appeared out of nowhere; then a girl with glowing eyes sniffed me; then the boys with glowing, exploding test tubes . . .* Cali almost started crying again, but with a deep breath and a sigh, she stopped the squeaking.

She had really never been a crier. When her cat, Lolly, died she didn't cry. She liked her cat, but it just didn't hurt that much to lose her. When Tony, a third grader from her old school, died last year in a car accident she didn't cry. It wasn't that she didn't care. It's just that she didn't know him very well.

Here she was crying over some surprises on a bus?

"Silly, silly, silly," she mumbled wiping her nose on the back of her hand. "Gross, gross, gross," she mumbled again as she wiped the back of her hand on her pants.

Mr. Fennelmyer negotiated a ninety degree turn to the right and then a ninety degree turn back to the left as the road made its way around the boundaries of somebody's hay field.

"You were saying, Cali?" Mr. Fennelmyer said, glancing in his rear-view mirror.

"I was saying—" She hesitated, leaned out in the aisle, and looked back. In the darkness she saw Shelley's blue eyes looking back at her. They blinked once. Embarrassed to be caught looking, Cali quickly turned back to the front. "I . . . I was saying that Shelley's eyes glow in the dark."

"Beautiful, aren't they?" said Mr. Fennelmyer. "I don't think I've ever met anyone with eyes that glowed like hers."

He's never met anyone else with glowing eyes? Or is it that he's met other people with glowing eyes, but not like hers?

It bothered her when people weren't clear in their meaning.

Always speak so as not to be misunderstood, said her lawyer father.

Her mother, also a lawyer, added, *Unless you* mean *to be misunderstood. Understand?*

Cali had to work hard to keep up with her mother's sense of humor.

Either way, it was clear Mr. Fennelmyer was not disturbed by glowing eyes. She wanted to talk about the strangeness of glowing eyes. She had a feeling that, with Mr. Fennelmyer, it would probably be like talking to a bird about the strangeness of being able to fly.

"Neither have I," Cali said. It seemed a safe answer. It was even true.

"Shelley doesn't have a lot of friends," Mr. Fennelmyer said.

That would be the glowing eyes and the sniffing, Cali thought.

"It's because she's shy," Mr. Fennelmyer went on.

Shy? How is her nose against my hand and her face in my space shy?

"If someone were to put in a little effort and patience with Shelley they would be rewarded with a loyal friend."

Cali glanced over her shoulder again. The eyes were still there, and still looking at her. *Having Shelley as a friend might be more of a problem than the good her loyalty will bring.*

The headlights lighted three boys standing at the end of a dirt lane. They looked about her age, eleven or twelve. Two were taller than the third boy. For boys, they looked average. Cali didn't like boys in that gossiping, whispering, giggling, note-passing way that some girls liked boys. Most boys were just stinky and clueless. A few were funny. She had met one who read comic books like *Batman,* and when he talked about them, he made them sound as important as the book *Moby Dick* was supposed to be. He was a genuinely interesting boy. He had moved.

As the bus stopped Cali noticed that the two taller boys were identical twins.

Two sets of twins on the bus. Great luck, she thought. She was glad to see none of them had lunch boxes with them.

When the doors opened Cali heard arguing voices.

"It just doesn't make sense for SpongeBob to look like a common kitchen sponge instead of an authentic sea sponge."

"It's true," said a second voice. "The whole SpongeBob concept came from artistic ideas about the intertidal zone. SpongeBob looking like a kitchen sponge is the same as making the stars seen in Star Trek have five little pointy arms as in children's books."

A third voice, exasperated, said, "Are you two immune to the subtleties of humor and metaphor? SpongeBob is a square. Square pants equals square personality. You can't put square pants on a sea sponge. Geez! Sometimes I can't believe we have the same mother."

At this point the three boys had climbed the steps and turned up the aisle. The first boy stopped suddenly at the sight of Cali. The other two boys ran into him. There was no sun yet, but the eastern horizon was bright with promise and enough light to see nearby faces.

"Look, it's a new girl," said the first boy.

"Hats off for the lady," said his twin.

All three took off imaginary hats and bowed with such serious grace that Cali blushed. She felt as if her face was glowing as brightly as Shelley's eyes.

"Let me introduce ourselves," said the first twin. He had dark eyes. Freckles ran across the bridge of his nose. "I am Bric. That's spelled B-R-I-C, if you please. This handsome fellow beside me is Frederick Douglas Fahr. Bringing up the rear is my esteemed, yet deluded, brother, Brac."

"That is spelled B-R-A-C," said the shorter fellow at the end.

"Wait," Cali said. "Don't you mean Frederick is your brother?"

"You can call me Freddy," Frederick interjected. "And, no, Bric and Brac are brothers. I'm just their friend."

"You two are brothers?" Cali said pointing at the tall one and short one. They looked nothing alike.

They nodded. Cali was suspicious. She thought she saw a smile on their lips. They were teasing the new girl.

"I'm not stupid," she said.

You must always follow the evidence, her father often said.

9

But evidence can be planted, and thus misleading, her mother always replied.

Between her two parents Cali felt perpetually confused.

"You two are identical twins," she said pointing to the two tall boys. "He doesn't look like anybody" she said pointing to Brac. Your joke is stupid."

"My name is Bric."

"And my name is Brac."

In unison they said, "With names like that you think we're not twin brothers?"

The voices in unison thing got to Cali. She was nearly convinced even though her eyes screamed to her brain that they were lying.

"Bric-a-brac," said Brac. Raising a finger he recited a dictionary definition. "Miscellaneous small articles collected for their antiquarian, sentimental, decorative, or other interest."

"Mom and Dad thought they were funny," said Bric. "You know, treating us like part of their collection."

Cali's brain was spinning. Looking at Freddy she asked, "How could you look so much like someone you aren't related to?"

Freddy shrugged. "*Doppelganger?*" he offered.

Doppelganger. Cali loved words. She had seen a YouTube video about a woman who had searched out her doppelgangers—strangers who looked remarkably like her.

"Take a seat," Mr. Fennelmyer said from behind the boys. "You're blowing my schedule."

"This bus has a way of making its *own* schedule," Brac said.

"Well, maybe that's true," Mr. Fennelmyer said, "but take a seat anyway."

"One more question," Bric said. "Where do you stand on the question of SpongeBob SquarePants?"

All three boys stared at her. She didn't like being pulled into their argument. SpongeBob didn't matter very much to Cali, but her mother loved the show. Cali sometimes sat with her during the show, but often brought a book to read at the same time.

They assume I know what they are talking about, Cali thought, *and that I care.* She wanted to just shrug and let it go, but three pairs of eyes stared at her expectantly. *Silly boys*, she thought.

When you don't know what to say, and you must say something, say something neutral, her father always said.

She cleared her throat. "SpongeBob sometimes makes me laugh."

"Ha, vindication," said Brac. "SpongeBob is funny."

"She said 'sometimes'," said Bric. "The lack of the scientific impedes the humor." They continued arguing as they moved toward the back of the bus.

Cali made a quick mental note that Bric was wearing a nice button-up shirt with SpongeBob embroidered on the shirt pocket. Freddy was wearing a brown t-shirt with Idaho Spud printed above a picture of a potato wearing a farmer's hat. That was the only way to tell them apart.

"Amazing, aren't they?" said Mr. Fennelmyer. "What are the odds of having two sets of twins on the bus at the same time?

Cali wondered if Mr. Fennelmyer meant the two twins who didn't look like each other or the two unrelated boys who were identical.

CHAPTER 3 – FELICIA'S FELINE MUFFINS

Once more the bus slowed to a stop. Cali watched as Mr. Fennelmyer pulled the air brake nob. There was a satisfying *pop* as the air brake engaged. He flicked a lever. *Hiss, clunk.* The doors opened. Outside everything was lit in a gray, pre-dawn light. The entire world had turned various shades of black and gray, like the old black and white movies her mom and dad enjoyed watching.

On the other side of a dry, scraggly lawn that was pushing through a layer of limp, dead leaves was a house. It was a dirty white square structure with a low, flat roof and nearly buried behind the bare limbs of lilac bushes. Half of the front window was hidden behind tall stalks of dead hollyhocks. On one side of the house a love swing hung from two A-frame supports. A gigantic cottonwood tree dwarfed the house and yard. A tire hung at the end of a rope attached to a limb thirty feet up. Cali imagined riding the tire in long, smooth arcs under the shade of that mammoth tree on hot summer afternoons.

Cali's mind colored the dead stalks and bare limbs. Come summer this would be one of those unkempt, overgrown, green places—the kind of place you might hope to see a fairy darting among snapdragons.

A ragged screen door shut with a bang as a girl exited the house. She was hidden underneath a stiff, scratchy, old-fashioned coat that hung below her knees. Cali's grandmother had worn coats like that. The girl had her hands in the pockets and the collar up around her neck.

Snug as a bug thought Cali.

The girl's frizzy hair billowed up and over the collar like an Arizona dust storm. *Completely uncontrollable*, Cali thought. *Poor girl.*

A shaggy cat ran out of the lilacs following her toward the bus. A second cat stepped out from behind the girl and walked beside her. A third cat scampered from the direction of the swing. They gave the girl a slinking feline escort.

A low growl sounded from inside the bus. Cali looked for the animal that made the sound. Shelley moved across the aisle and pressed both hands against the window. She was focused on the cats. Cali shivered as she heard Shelley growl again.

"Shelley," Mr. Fennelmyer called, looking up into the mirror. "Get back in your seat."

Shelley obeyed, backing away slowly, keeping her eyes on the cats for as long as possible.

"Is she okay?" Cali asked. She wondered that somebody—anybody—let Shelley go to school

"Don't let her fool you," Mr. Fennelmyer said, "she loves cats."

"That's not what I—"

Mr. Fennelmyer cut her off, "She got out here once. The cats led her on the chase of her life. Her clothes were torn and she was filthy when we finally got her back on the bus. She was as happy as I've ever seen her." He looked out the door thoughtfully. "I think the cats keep hoping she'll come out again."

The girl climbed onto the bus leaving the cats twitching their tails at the bottom of the steps. When she turned to move up the aisle she came to an abrupt halt when she saw Cali. The smell of cigarette smoke and, Cali sniffed again, yes, it was cat, drifted by.

"A new girl?" the girl asked. Her voice was clear and happy like a meadowlark's song.

"It's been a while, hasn't it, Felicia?" said Mr. Fennelmyer.

"Will she keep riding with us?" She stared at Cali with hope on her face. Her eyes were blue, like Shelley's, but they didn't glow. They did sparkle just a little, especially when she smiled. Silver braces festooned her teeth. Close up Cali could see that there was an order to Felicia's wild hair. It had been brushed. There was even a hairclip with the face of a kitten placed carefully in the mass near the top of her head. Each strand of hair seemed to demand its own space making all of it appear to float around her head. There was something—Cali searched for the word—something *magnificent* about her hair. Maybe it was the totally unapologetic way that Felicia wore it.

"I don't think she's decided yet," Mr. Fennelmyer said.

Disappointment flashed through Felicia's eyes. She reached under her coat and pulled out something wrapped in a napkin. "Here," she said, handing it to Cali. "I hope you'll decide to ride with us." She moved on, but then looked over her shoulder directly into Cali's eyes. "Forever," she added.

Felicia spoke with disturbing sincerity. She seemed like the kind of girl who might decide that Cali needed a friend and try to sit by her at lunch.

You can never have too many friends, Cali's mother always said.

Just make sure they are the right kind, her father would add.

Felicia was the kind of friend who might make being the new girl at school harder, not easier. She was that strange kind of girl who didn't know she was strange.

That's not what I meant, she imagined her father saying. Cali ignored him.

Cali unwrapped the napkin to discover a homemade blueberry muffin. It warmed the palm of her hand as if it had just come out of the oven. Butter dripped from where the muffin had been split and then put back together.

"If you're not going to eat that . . ." Mr. Fennelmyer said, glancing at it with hopeful eyes.

"What is it?" Cali asked. She knew what it was, but why was it sitting in her hand? The aroma of blueberries and muffin reached her nose and her mouth watered. Still, her mind rebelled at the idea of eating unpackaged food pulled out from under a stranger's coat, especially one that smelled like cigarettes and cat.

"It's Felicia's breakfast. She gave it to you."

"It's her breakfast?"

"She has one every morning on the bus. She loves blueberries."

"I can't eat her breakfast," Cali said, resolutely. "I've got to give it back."

Mr. Fennelmyer braked to a quick stop. Cali almost slid off her seat.

"No!" Mr. Fennelmyer said. It sounded like he was talking to a naughty puppy.

"Mr. Aagard's pigs in the road again?" Freddy called.

"No pigs," Mr. Fennelmyer hollered. Embarrassed, he took his foot off the break and let the bus start rolling again

Cali bristled. "She'll be hungry," she said.

"That's the point of her gift."

"She wants to be hungry?"

"Nobody wants to be hungry."

"My point exactly." Cali felt vindicated.

Mr. Fennelmyer wasn't done yet. "Felicia's *point exactly* was to be kind to you. If she didn't give you something that she really wanted, she would only be nice, not kind."

What? Cali thought? *He's changing the subject.* She was curious. "What's wrong with being nice?"

"Nothing if it's all you're capable of. But Felicia is capable of great kindness—I think it's her superpower. For her to make a gift of something that didn't really matter to her would be like . . . like," he struggled for an example. "Like a billionaire giving away nickels to the poor." He slapped the steering wheel as if he had just nailed the simile.

Cali looked back to see if Felicia could hear them talking about her. She saw Shelley's head zip back from the aisle. Felicia was sitting next to her. They probably couldn't hear.

"Well," Cali said, unwilling to give in to Mr. Fennelmyer's reasoning, "if I eat Felicia's breakfast I won't even be being nice," she said, stumbling over her words. She could see her father shaking his head with his hand over his face.

"There's no doubt in the whole entire world that you can be nice," Mr. Fennelmyer said. "The question is, can you be kind?"

Mr. Fennelmyer unsettled Cali. It had started the moment the bus doors opened. Everyone else on the bus seemed to be at ease with him. *Why is he picking on me?. It's because I don't know who I am, that's why.*

"I can be kind," she said, hoping it was true.

"Then eat the muffin," Mr. Fennelmyer said. "It would mean the world to her."

"It would?"

Mr. Fennelmyer nodded. "She gives out so much kindness and gets very little back."

Cali recalled Felicia's hair, her braces, her sincerity, and her old coat. She thought she understood. Looking at the muffin Cali imagined Felicia imagining her eating it. Mentally turning off her gag reflex, she took a bite. It was cold now. The butter wasn't butter, but margarine. Underneath the blueberry and muffin and margarine there were the faintest hints of cigarette smoke and . . . cat?

Felicia's sparkling eyes came to mind. "Will she ever give up on being kind?" The question danced like a spark from Cali's brain to her tongue. She heard the words before she realized she was speaking.

"I don't think she will," Mr. Fennelmyer said. "That's probably why she can ride this bus."

Cali took another bite and struggled to swallow. *This 'being kind' thing might kill me.*

CHAPTER 4 – THE PIPES OF JIMMY BACKMAN

Cali knew how to keep from breathing through her nose while eating. She learned a long time ago she could eat almost anything that way. If you can't smell it, you can't taste it. Some kids had to plug their nose with their fingers to achieve this. Not Cali. She could close the passage to her nose at the back of her throat just by thinking about it. She could even eat her Aunt Pat's liverwurst stew without offending her.

The muffin wasn't all that bad. In fact it was almost delicious. Then that hint of cigarettes and cat snuck in and ruined everything. Cali looked over her shoulder to see Felicia three seats back sitting next to Shelley. She was singing a happy song in what sounded like French, bobbing her head side to side to the beat. Shelley listened and grinned.

Cali put the last bite in her mouth and swallowed without chewing. She grimaced as the piece of muffin made its way slowly down her throat.

"I like her muffins," Mr. Fennelmyer said.

It had been three miles since he had spoken. He seemed to have muffins on his mind.

"Felicia gives me her muffin on my birthday."

Cali realized that Mr. Fennelmyer could see her in his inside, rear-view mirror. She could just see his eyes at the bottom of the mirror from where she sat. He had been watching her eat the muffin. She blushed realizing he had probably seen her grimace on that last bite.

If you don't like the line of questioning, change the line, her father always said.

You should see him try that when I ask him if these pants make me look fat, said her mother.

"Mr. Fennelmyer, you said something a while ago."

"Figures. I can't keep my big mouth shut."

"When you talked about kindness, you said, 'That's why Felicia can ride this bus.' What did you mean by that?"

"I didn't say that."

"You did."

"I said, 'That's probably why.' There's a difference."

"No, there's not."

"Yes, there is."

Cali felt unusually feisty. At home her parents would often spar with words, attack each other's line of reasoning, find weaknesses in points of view. They, her father mostly, would try to bait Cali into these arguments. She was skilled at letting things go. Mr. Fennelmyer—the most unlawyer-like, plain-looking, ordinary man she had ever seen— brought the feisty out of her without even trying. Maybe not trying was the difference.

"Do you mean if she wasn't kind she couldn't ride this bus? And if that's what you meant, then who is the judge who allowed her to ride?" As the words left her mouth Cali felt the thrill of having asked the perfect question. A perfect question was one so sharp that it stripped a person of all defenses and left them standing there naked, so to speak. Anyway, that's what her father told her.

Mr. Fennelmyer stared speechless at Cali in the mirror. Not satisfied with a reflection, he turned and stared at her directly for a moment before going back to the mirror.

"You say both your parents are lawyers?" he finally said. "It shows."

Cali thought a moment, satisfied by his reaction to her perfect question, until she realized he had just changed the subject. She had never told him anything about her parents.

"How did you know my parents were lawyers?"

"I didn't know."

"You just said you could tell my parents were lawyers."

"I was guessing."

Frustrated, Cali sat and steamed for a moment. Was Mr. Fennelmyer teasing? Was he lying? Was he supernatural? That last question made her pause. She finally decided that whatever he was, he knew things.

The bus came to a stop in front of three derelict, cement grain silos. A slightly pudgy boy in plaid shorts and white gym socks stood with one hand tucked into the pocket of his blue jacket. The other hand held the handle of a black briefcase.

"Morning, Mr. Fennelmyer," he said in a high voice as he clomped up the steps.

"Looking good, Jimmy," Mr. Fennelmyer said.

"Yeah, the socks are brand new." He saw Cali and sucked in a breath of surprise. "A new rider," he exclaimed, as he studied her.

Didn't your mother teach you not to stare? Sensing another set of eyes behind her, she glanced back and saw Shelley's eyes dart back down behind the seat in front of her.

"Excuse me, Mr. Fennelmyer," Jimmy said, "but do you really think she belongs on this bus?"

"Her name is Cali," Mr. Fennelmyer said. "Cali, this is Jimmy Backman."

"It's pronounced *Bach*man," Jimmy said, emphasizing the first syllable, "as in Johann Sebastian Bach. You've heard of him, I presume?"

There was something cute about the way he stood straighter and raised his chin when he said this. Cali wanted to pinch his pudgy cheeks. He looked like he was only in third grade.

"Yes, Bach," she said. "'Toccata and Fugue in D Minor'. I love it."

"She hasn't decided if she is going to ride this bus yet," Mr. Fennelmyer said, answering Jimmy's original question.

Jimmy's mouth had fallen open when Cali had said "Toccata and Fugue" and stayed that way as Mr. Fennelmyer spoke.

"And your parents pronounce it *Back*man," Mr. Fennelmyer added.

Jimmy ignored him. He stood there with a look of adoration in his eyes. "I hope you will ride with us forever and ever."

With a look of rapture on his face he disappeared up the aisle.

"You may be sorry you told him that," Mr. Fennelmyer said with a grunt, as he released the air brake.

"Why?"

"Never mind." he said, "There are some ear protectors under your seat."

Cali felt rather proud to be able to name that piece. Of course it was one of Bach's most famous works. It also happened to be the only organ work by Bach that Cali knew by name. Like most girls her age she was most familiar with the current pop songs. It's just that *Toccata and Fugue* was one of the featured works on her father's old cd's from the music appreciation class he took as a freshman in college. When he pulled out his old cd's and listened to 'Toccata and Fugue' he would act like he was the Hunchback of Notre Dame playing the organ.

The Hunchback is only known for the bells of Notre Dame, her mother would say, drolly, pointing out her father's theatrical error. She put her hand over her ears and quoted, *The bells! The bells!*

The Hunchback had secret music ninja skills, returned her father, bent over, and pounding invisible keys as the music swelled.

Behind her Cali heard the sound of construction. There was clicking, clinking, and tapping. One sound followed another as if somebody was building something they had built many times before. By the time she turned around an array of silver and gold metal tubes were sticking up from behind a seat. Organ pipes? That's what they had to be. They fanned out like a peacock's tail feathers and were almost as beautiful. They shone in the early morning light.

She guessed it was Jimmy who sat behind those pipes. She only saw hands reach above the seat as more pipes were fit together. Where were they coming from? His briefcase?

He's pulling a full-blown pipe organ out of his briefcase.

Cali turned around and sat down. It was clear that she was dreaming. Cali pinched herself. Hard. "Owww," she said, rubbing her arm. She looked back over the top of her seat again to see even more pipes.

Across the aisle Felicia and Shelley were sitting unperturbed, both wearing red hearing protectors that fit over the top of the head. Felicia saw Cali looking and pretended the hearing protectors were headphones and that she was listening to rock music.

Awkward and embarrassing, Cali thought.

Cali turned to Mr. Fennelmyer hoping that he would say something to make sense of it all.

"I warned you," was all he said. He reached under his seat and pulled out his own personal pair of hearing protectors. He struggled to put them on as he drove.

Cali felt under her seat. She touched the bottom of the seat carefully, afraid she might find used chewing gum. Instead she felt a little shelf. From it she pulled out red ear protectors. Mr. Fennelmyer nodded at her from the driver's seat and pointed to his.

Confused, Cali peered back over the seats again just in time to see dust puff from one of the pipes. A hollow *Toooot* sounded as a single note was played. It wasn't very loud, so Cali didn't put on her ear protection.

She heard some more clinking and tapping as Jimmy made adjustments. Another *toooot* sounded—the same note as the previous toot. This one didn't come from Jimmy's pipes, but from the back of the bus. A thin column of green gas floated up from Marty's and Marcus's seat.

Jimmy stuck his head into the aisle. "What!" he yelled.

Marty leaned into the aisle in a challenge. "You heard me."

In the driver's seat Mr. Fennelmyer pulled down his ear protectors. "Oh, Cali, I am so sorry you have to endure this on your first day."

"Endure what?" Cali said.

"Toot war!" yelled Bric, Brac, and Freddy.

Jimmy looked at Cali with adoration still in his eyes. "As fifth graders they should know better than to challenge me, but I must do what I must do."

Another toot sounded about two notes lower than the last. Cali saw the pipe vibrate.

Cali heard mumbling and movement in the back of the bus. "No, that is D# not D," one of the twins said in a raised voice.

"Amateurs," Jimmy said, looking at Cali and indicating the twins in the back with a jerk of his head.

Toot. More gas appeared in back. It was the exact same note that Jimmy had played, but a little louder.

"But not bad for chemists," Mr. Fennelmyer said over his shoulder.

Jimmy pursed his lips and narrowed his eyes, annoyed by the truth of Mr. Fennelmyer's statement. His head disappeared behind his pipes. An instant later, an entire octave lower, an immense *Tooooot* rolled out.

Cali felt her seat vibrate so much that it tickled her bottom. She put her hands over her ears, but the note had already ended.

"Oh, yeah," yelled Bric with great satisfaction.

"That's what I'm talking about," added Brac.

"What are you two going to do about it?" taunted Freddy.

"Don't even try it," Jimmy yelled.

Marcus stood up so he could be seen over the seats. "We will not be denied!"

He disappeared behind the seat and there were sounds of mixing and pouring and arguing. Words floated up to the front: *Double low F# . . . bottle . . . not big enough . . . screw it on tight . . . I'm afraid.*

"I'm the adult. I should stop this," Mr. Fennelmyer muttered.

Whether he actually decided to act or not could never be determined. At the back of the bus two hands appeared above the seat holding a large jar. A thick column of green smoke streamed up through a hole in the lid. As the smoke streamed thicker and faster a rumble sounded that started to resolve into the same note Jimmy had played. As it grew in volume Cali desperately tried to put on her ear protection. Before she could finish there was a dull *Boom.* The lid ricocheted off the ceiling with a ping, bounced off two seats, then rolled up the aisle, finally falling over when it reached the garbage can in front.

"Fools," shouted Jimmy, kneeling on his seat, looking back at Marty and Marcus. "You dare to challenge the Bach Man—"

He would have gone on if he hadn't started gagging and coughing. Green gas filled the bus. Cali held her breath as the gas enveloped her. She looked at Mr. Fennelmyer with wide, frightened eyes.

"It's not poisonous," he said, sliding his window open, "but it's not pleasant either." To himself he muttered, "I'm gonna have to take their chemistry set away from them for a couple of days."

Cali held her breath and was determined to pass out before she breathed in the green gas. She didn't succeed. She involuntarily gulped in a breath and gagged on the smell of warm, bologna sandwiches.

"Believe me, it could be worse," Mr. Fennelmyer said, throwing her an 'I've been there' glance. "Windows down," he yelled over the intercom.

Bric, Brac, and Freddy spread out on one side of the bus, while Felicia and Shelley took the other side. Windows clicked down and cold, morning air gushed in making the gas whirl and swirl.

Above the sound of the rushing wind a high pitched laugh pealed.

"Ha Ha Ha Ha Ha,"

It was Jimmy, still glorying in his victory.

"It's too late to talk him down," Mr. Fennelmyer yelled. "For heaven's sake, put on your ear protection."

The others dived for their seats. Still gagging on the smell of warm bologna Cali pulled on her ear protectors just in time. Jimmy hit the magnificent, overwhelming opening chords of Bach's *Toccata and Fugue in D Minor*. The bus interior became fluid with the vibrations as Jimmy rolled down to the low notes of the scale. The windows jiggled their way back up and then down again as the notes rolled out. Cali realized she wasn't listening to organ music as much as she was floating in it.

Is it possible to drown in music?

Outside an entire herd of cows raised their heads as the yellow machine rolled past. Wondering at the rumbling, they curiously raised their noses to the trail of green gas it left behind.

Chapter 5 – Don't Make Me Turn On The Radio

The last notes of the fugue echoed into silence and Cali landed gently on her seat.

Was I really floating or just out of my mind?

Cold wind slapped her face, bringing her back to her senses.

Oh, yes, the music, she thought. She remembered the windows jiggling up and down to the low notes. It had been like a dream. The whole morning was a dream.

"Here, let me get that for you."

Cali opened her eyes to see Felicia leaning over her to reach the window.

Still dreaming, Cali thought. Her arm ached where she had pinched it earlier.

Her mouth full of braces, Felicia flashed Cali a silvery smile as the window clacked up. "The windows do this every time Jimmy plays one of the big pieces by Bach. We can never guess if there will be more windows down than up. It was a tie today."

After Felicia had moved on to another window Cali realized she should have thanked her for the muffin.

Mr. Fennelmyer pulled off his ear protectors. Glancing over his shoulder, he yelled, "Jimmy, let me be the first to tell you that you've never played better."

A smattering of applause sounded around the bus.

"It was like you were inspired," Fennelmyer went on.

Cali looked back as Jimmy stood and took a bow. He looked at her with bright, expectant eyes. Still shaken by the musical experience Cali closed her eyes and sat back in her seat. She heard Felicia say, "You did great, Jimmy," and realized that he had been hoping for a word of approval from her. Cali looked back, but Jimmy had already sat down behind his pipes.

Shelley, across the aisle and one seat behind Jimmy, was watching Jimmy work with his pipes. She looked up and met Cali's eyes. Neither one turned away. It was light now and Shelley's eyes had lost their glow. She was a plain-looking girl with unkempt brown hair and a black bow on the side. Shelley looked at Cali like there was something she wanted to say. Before she could say it Felicia returned and sat beside Shelley, distracting her.

Cali wished someone would sit next to her. Maybe they could explain this bus, or, if they couldn't, it would just be nice to have a warm body near. It was unlikely to happen because she didn't make friends. It took too much work to have friends. When you were with friends you had to be careful what you said. You had to pretend to like things you didn't like. To have friends you had to be someone you weren't just so you could fit in.

There is a price for friendship, said her mother. *But some friends are worth their weight in gold.*

Others pay far too much for inferior goods, added her father.

Cali had never wanted to pay the price. Her friendship cupboard remained bare. Normally she was okay with that. She liked her own company well enough, but today her self-confidence was wavering. She needed some support.

Up ahead Cali saw a group of kids waiting beside the road in front of a line of houses. Three girls stood talking while four boys were pushing and shoving each other in horseplay. The bus passed by them without slowing down. The turbulence caused by the bus ruffled their hair, but they didn't even look up.

"Didn't you miss those kids?" Cali asked.

"Nope," replied Mr. Fennelmyer.

"They looked like they were waiting for the bus."

"They get on the other bus."

"There's more than one bus? Mom didn't tell me that."

"Doesn't matter."

"But what if I got on the wrong bus?"

Mr. Fennelmyer took his hat off and ran his hand through his hair. Now that Cali could see him she wanted to run her hand through his hair, too. He had one of the sharpest, shortest flat tops she had ever seen. She could imagine the stiff, soft, pokiness on the palm of her hand. She also noticed he wore suspenders. Sometimes Cali's dad wore suspenders, red ones. When he did he also wore a matching red bowtie.

Why do you sometimes wear suspenders and a bowtie?

Just on special days, he always answered. He would never tell her what made the days special.

"Almost never happens," said Mr. Fennelmyer, bring Cali back to the present.

"Why not?"

"You get on the bus that stops for you."

That didn't make sense. In Salt Lake City several buses might stop at one stop. A person had to know which bus to get on. Mr. Fennelmyer was saying that out here the bus wouldn't stop unless it was the right bus.

"You knew I was going to start riding today?"

Mr. Fennelmyer glanced at her uneasily. "No."

"And yet you stopped for me. Why?"

"Why do you ask so many questions?" Mr. Fennelmyer sounded grumpy.

Answering a question with a question is a good way to redirect the conversation. Cali's mother taught her this.

Oh, no you don't, thought Cali. "Would the other bus have stopped for me if you hadn't?"

Mr. Fennelmyer gave her a sulky glance. "Yes."

"So why did *you* stop for me?"

Mr. Fennelmyer looked defeated, but then his face lit up with an idea. "The question isn't why I stopped; it's why did you get on." He looked at her and smiled. "You remember you had a choice."

Cali slunk back in her seat. It looked like he had her. And he still hadn't answered her question.

"But why did you stop for me?" She folded her arms stubbornly. "It's a simple question. I demand an answer."

Mr. Fennelmyer glanced at her—annoyed? No, his look was more troubled. "Not all simple questions have simple answers," he mumbled.

That caught Cali off guard. Her dad often told her the same thing. Her stubbornness faded and she decided that maybe she'd just forget it for now.

Mr. Fennelmyer continued, "I didn't stop for you this morning; the bus did."

Hmm, she thought. Her mind moved into criminal investigation mode. *What is Mr. Fennelmyer up to? Could be it that he's teasing me—jerking me around, as Dad puts it. A bus doesn't drive itself. More likely he only meant that he had forgotten that he was supposed to pick me up and had to stop sudde—*

Cali cut that thought short. She went back to the first thought. What she had already seen on this bus defied explanation. Her sore arm kept her from returning to the dream theory. She decided to continue the line of interrogation.

"So, you're telling me this bus doesn't really need you, that it does what it wants?"

"Well," Mr. Fennelmyer said, struggling for words, "let's just say it doesn't need me any more than a horse needs a rider."

"But a horse doesn't need a rider," Cali said.

"You ever seen a horse look like it had anything important to do when it didn't have a rider?"

They were passing a field with two horses in it. One was standing doing its three-legged sleep thing while the other was lazily searching the barren ground for something to nibble on.

"Okay," Cali conceded. "I still don't get it."

Mr. Fennelmyer threw her a glance, drummed his fingers on the steering wheel, and finally said, "Guess I'll just have to show you. Come stand by me."

Cali's curiosity needle hit *maximum* as she got up and stood by the driver's seat.

Mr. Fennelmyer pointed and said, "That's Kadlin Harrison up there. He doesn't ride this bus."

About a quarter mile up the road Cali saw the figure of a boy waiting at the end of a dirt lane.

"Look through the visor." Mr. Fennelmyer lowered the green plastic visor that's normally used to keep the sun out of the driver's eyes.

Cali looked. Kadlin looked the way he should when viewed through a green plastic visor.

"So?" she said.

"Now look up there." He pointed into the sky.

Cali bent over so she could look up through the visor. "Whoa." There was something shining there. It was smaller than the moon, but far brighter than a star. It was like looking at Jupiter in the night sky.

Mr. Fennelmyer pushed up the visor. "Now look."

"It's gone," Cali said.

"Look harder," Mr. Fennelmyer said.

Cali squinted. After a moment she saw a speck in the sky. "You mean that dot up there?"

"That's Veronica Dover. She rides this bus." He lowered the visor and once again there was the glow that surrounded the dot.

Cali forgot the original question as a thousand new questions popped into her head. First was *What is Veronica doing up there?*

Mr. Fennelmyer held to the original subject. "When I first saw you this morning you looked a lot like Kadlin through the visor, but then you flickered once or twice almost as bright as Veronica. I figured there was something wrong with the visor and was going to pass you by. The bus had other ideas and came to a rather sudden stop."

"It knocked my chemistry set off my lap," Marty said from directly behind her.

"I fell off my seat," added Shelley, in a quiet voice.

Cali spun around to find that all the other kids on the bus had moved to the front and were crowed in the aisle and seats behind her.

"What?" Mr. Fennelmyer said, looking up into his mirror. "Get back to your seats."

"We never get to look through the visor," said Bric.

"Never," echoed Brac.

"How does the new girl rate?" asked Marty.

"She asked the right questions," said Mr. Fennelmyer, "something you have yet to learn the value of."

"What?" said Marcus. "When you know as much as me you don't have to ask many questions. Can she recite the Periodic Table frontwards and backwards in twenty-six and a half seconds?"

Mr. Fennelmyer gave Cali a questioning look. Cali shook her head. Having cleared that up, he went on. "And yet it was her willingness to ask questions that got her a look through the visor. If I've told you once I've told you a hundred times, progress is made from questions, not answers."

. . . from questions, not answers, several of the kids said, in unison with Mr. Fennelmyer as if they had heard the quote a hundred times.

"Yeah," said Marty, backhanding Marcus's shoulder. "Why don't you come up with a half intelligent question for once?"

"Like, 'Where's the ketchup?' wasn't the last question I heard you ask," responded Marcus.

"'Where's the ketchup?' is a perfectly good question if you need the ketchup," said Felicia, reassuring Marty.

Cali saw that Marcus had a smart response to Felicia's statement. He opened his mouth, looked at Felicia's silvery smile, and then reconsidering, said, "Of course you're right."

Felicia nodded.

"Ketchup smetchup," said Mr. Fennelmyer. "If you don't all get back to your seats in three seconds, I'm turning on the radio."

The sudden silence was deafening. Cali looked at the others. Jimmy looked like he had grabbed hold of an electric fence. The others looked like they had drunk sour milk.

"*Pop* music," Jimmy said, when he finally got his jaw to move.

"Yes, pop music," said Mr. Fennelmyer. "Wouldn't hurt any of you to stay conversant on current affairs."

"And radio hosts with their insipid banter?" asked Marcus.

"I can't bring myself to believe that commercial radio hosts are as stupid as they sound," Bric said.

"And yet 'stupid is as stupid speaks,'" answered Brac.

"The obnoxious commercials rot a person from the inside out," added Freddy.

Mr. Fennelmyer reached for the radio.

They screamed and scurried up the aisle to their seats.

Cali sat down again, too. She wasn't nearly as afraid of the radio as the others. Sshe felt dissatisfied and realized it was because she had more questions now than before she asked her first question.

They passed Kadlin. He never even looked up from his iPad. The road was narrow and Kadlin stood right at the edge of it. Only three feet separated him from the bus. Strange that Kadlin didn't flinch as the bus passed so near.

"How come they don't look at us?" she said, to no one in particular. She pushed her head against the window to keep Kadlin in view.

"You don't ride this bus; you don't see this bus," said Felicia as she passed by. She had come up to get Mr. Fennelmyer's box of tissues for Jimmy. He was wiping down his pipes as he put them away.

Mr. Fennelmyer, glancing at her in his mirror, raised his eyebrows and tilted his head in a way that said, *It's true, but don't ask right now.*

Cali would have asked anyway if she hadn't been distracted by what she saw in the sky. Mr. Fennelmyer had pushed the visor back up. The speck in the sky was clearly visible now. It was a parachute with a person dangling below.

"Right on time, as usual," Mr. Fennelmyer said, checking his watch.

Chapter 6 – The Historic Arrival of Veronica Dover

"She's trying to catch the bus?" Cali asked.

Who parachutes out of the sky to catch a school bus? How many elementary students parachute at all? Was this even allowed? Did her parents know?

"Your question is more accurate than you know," said Mr. Fennelmyer. "In fact, today might be the day." Grabbing the intercom microphone, he yelled, "Landing crew!"

Bric, Brac, and Freddy leapt to their feet.

"Really?" Bric said.

"You think she's going to do it today?" asked Brac.

"Go! Go! Go!" Freddy yelled, tiring of the questions and pushing Bric and Brac into the aisle. "Do it how we trained."

Freddy ran up to the front ceiling emergency exit. He climbed onto the seats so he could reach it. Cali watched as he turned the lever from "Locked" to "Release."

"I want to help," said Jimmy, standing next to his seat.

"This is strictly sixth grade work," Freddy said. "Remain in your seat."

Pushing with all his might Freddy lifted the hatch on its hinges and swiveled it out of the way. Cali saw pale blue sky through the hatch and felt the rush of cold air. In the back Bric and Brac completed the same task with considerable more arguing over who got to do what.

"What are they doing?" Cali said, looking at Mr. Fennelmyer.

"Can't talk," he muttered while leaning forward and peering into the sky to where Veronica dangled.

The bus sped ahead. The air whooshed through the open hatch.

Cali looked at Freddy. "What is *he* doing?" she asked, motioning with her thumb toward the driver.

Freddy was trying to balance himself as he climbed on top of a seat.

"We have to get close enough before Veronica gets too low." He wobbled as he stood and reached for the edge of the hatch. Once he had hold he straddled the aisle with a foot on top of a seat on either side. He could just put his head through the hatch into the wind outside.

"Yeeeehawwwwww," he yelled. Looking toward the back he said, "Oh, hi, Bric and Brac. Fancy meeting you here."

Cali looked back to see both Bric and Brac's heads disappearing through the hatch. Like Freddy, Bric could just reach. Brac was too short. His legs dangled as he leaned forward on his arms on top of the bus. There wasn't enough room for two. They squeezed together uncomfortably in the hatch.

"Only one of you is supposed to be in the hatch," Freddy yelled.

"Yeah, and it's *my* turn," they both yelled back.

"Would you quit arguing and tell me where I am?" Mr. Fennelmyer shouted.

"Stop," Freddy shouted. "You're passing her."

Cali heard the brakes squeal and was thrown against the seat in front of her.

Oof, Freddy said, as he struggled to keep his balance.

There was a *thump* in the back of the bus as Brac lost his grip and fell into the aisle. He muttered something grumpily.

"Thank you, Mr. Fennelmyer," Bric called from outside, his voice muted.

Everything went quiet as the bus came to a stop in the middle of the narrow country road.

"Is that an airport?" Cali said, looking out the west side windows. There was a large sheet metal building with a premanufactured structure sitting near it. She could see three or four small airplanes sitting on the tarmac. There wasn't a soul in sight. A white and green light rotated on a striped pole nearby.

"It's the Warburton Municipal Airport," Felicia said.

"That's why this road is called 'Airport Road'" Shelley added in her low, husky voice.

Sitting next to Felicia, Shelley seemed almost normal. Of course, there were still her amazingly bright blue eyes, a strange voice, and the odd way she stared at her—Cali decided that maybe she was still a little creepy.

"Her parents used to land here so that Veronica could catch the bus," Felicia explained. "But they decided it was faster for Veronica to just jump out."

"Her parents fly an airplane here? Where do they live?

"Just in the mountains over there," Felicia said, pointing to the low, bare mountains rising a few miles behind the airport. "There are no roads, but they have a little landing strip."

"Wolves live in those mountains," Shelley said, staring out the window at them. Her voice was almost a growl.

Cali felt goosebumps run up her back.

"But if she is just going to jump out, why doesn't she jump out over the school?" asked Cali.

"It's miles out of the way," said Felicia.

"And it's against school rules," added Jimmy.

"If it's against the rules at school, isn't it against the rules on the bus?" Cali asked.

"This is Bus 13," Shelley said softly.

Apparently Bus 13 being Bus 13 explained everything perfectly.

"Okay, start coasting forward," called Freddy, his head still outside the hatch.

The air brakes squelched and the bus rolled forward.

Cali put her face up against her window trying to catch sight of Veronica, but she couldn't see directly above the bus.

Mom, a little girl is landing on the bus in a parachute, she thought.

Such an imagination, her mom replied.

Exactly, Cali thought. *My imagination. What was in my Fruit Loops this morning?*

"A little faster," called Freddy.

"Come on, Ronni!" yelled Bric, cheering from his observation post at the back of the bus.

"Is she really going to do it this time?" asked Marcus. He was standing in the aisle next to Bric's legs, trying to look up out of the hatch.

"Do you know what the odds are?" said Marty. He had a calculator in his hands.

"I don't care about the odds," Brac said. He leapt out of his seat and began trying to climb up Bric's legs to the hatch. "All I know is that Ronni and Mr. Fennelmyer need my help."

"Leggo," Bric yelled, kicking his legs. "Oh my gosh, here she comes."

"Easy. Eaaaasy," Freddy called, to Mr. Fennelmyer, or Veronica, or maybe it was both. "Oh, crap!"

Freddy tumbled to the aisle floor as a figure in a white jumpsuit and helmet slipped through the hatch and landed right on top of him. A moment later the figure shot back up to the hatch, pulled by the parachute cords, where she hit her head with a *thump.*

"Stop the bus," Bric yelled. "The wind's got her parachute."

Mr. Fennelmyer hit the brakes.

As the bus slowed the air left the parachute. Veronica fell again, once more landing on Freddy. Cali heard, *Oof,* from Freddy and a crash at the back of the bus.

"If my chemistry set falls off my lap one more time . . ." Marty complained.

The bus idled in the middle of the road. For an instant, silence reigned. All eyes were on the girl in white.

"Hi, Ronni," Freddy said as he lay on his back in the aisle.

Veronica stood straddling him awkwardly. "Hello, Freddy," she said. "Thanks for the soft landing . . . twice." She was rubbing the side of her face as she spoke.

"Are you all right?" Mr. Fennelmyer asked. "I apologize for not stopping in time. They don't cover this kind of thing in bus driver class."

Brac and the others made their way to the front. Brac's mouth hung. He couldn't believe what he was hearing.

"*Hi Ronni?*" he said looking at Freddy. "*I apologize?*" he said looking at Mr. Fennelmyer. "Don't any of you realize that we finally did it? How many times have we tried and failed? We finally did it!"

The bus came to life.

"Hurrah!" shouted Jimmy. "Hurrah! Hurrah!"

In the back Marty was shaking a jar filled with more green gas. Pressure built up and something like silly string started squirting through a hole in the top. It was accompanied by a whistling sound. Freddy got up and started doing a herky-jerky jig with Bric and Brac. Felicia smiled and clapped. Mr. Fennelmyer, looking pleased as punch, offered Cali knuckles. Shelley raised her head and howled. Cali, the only one on the bus still sitting, just stared at the scene.

During all this Veronica calmly took off her helmet. A mop of curly, orange hair fell down around her face. It was almost fluorescent against the white of her jumpsuit. Cali noticed freckles covered her pudgy, round cheeks. Her eyes were green and clear as the sky. She was short, plump, and couldn't have been any older than fourth grade.

Veronica noticed Cali staring and stared boldly back.

"A new girl," she said, surprised. "Mr. Fennelmyer, I didn't know we were getting a new girl."

"Neither did I," he answered.

She studied Cali a moment longer. "Are you sure she's supposed to be on this bus?"

Mr. Fennelmyer, uncomfortable speaking about Cali right in front of her, looked at her as he said, "I believe it's up to her. She has to decide."

"Well, that's unusual," Veronica said.

"Indeed. It's unprecedented," chimed in Marcus.

"Unprecedented," muttered Mr. Fennelmyer. "Show off."

"Not at all," said Marcus. "It's exactly what I mean. The right word is never the wrong word. Right?"

"Oh, just get her parachute in here and go sit down," Mr. Fennelmyer said, waving all the kids away with his hand. "We still have a ways to go."

"Don't forget pizza," said Bric, as he started pulling the cords through the hatch.

"Pizza? What about pizza?" asked Mr. Fennelmyer.

"You promised us a pizza party when we finally caught Veronica through the hatch," said Brac. He was straddling the aisle on seatbacks now, guiding the material of the parachute through the hatch.

"Oh, I never—" began Mr. Fennelmyer, but Brac stopped what he was doing and pulled a small digital recorder out of his pocket and pressed the 'play' button. It was a noisy recording, but Mr. Fennelmyer's voice was clear enough:

That was close this time. You know, if we ever do catch Veronica through the hatch I'll spring for pizza.

"What? You recorded that?" said Mr. Fennelmyer. He didn't look pleased.

"Your memory isn't what it used to be," Brac said, trying to suppress a grin.

"Well,. I remember now. I'll see what I can do." Mr. Fennelmyer plopped down in the driver's seat looking annoyed.

"Pepperoni," called out Jimmy.

"And sausage, and bacon, and ham, and chicken," said Shelley, saliva running down the corner of her mouth.

She would have gone on, but Felicia interrupted her. "You have such good taste."

Shelley smiled and wiped drool from her chin.

Veronica unstrapped the harness. Freddy and Bric, arms full, took the parachute to an empty seat and shoved it in. Veronica peeled off the white jumpsuit revealing a denim skirt and black leggings underneath. The denim skirt was wrinkled from having been bunched up inside the jumpsuit. Cali hadn't expected a skirt.

Veronica caught her staring. "Mom wonders why I insist on skirts, too," she said. "It's just that they make me feel like a woman."

These words, spoken so sincerely from such a young girl, made Cali smile.

Veronica came forward in all her orangeness and stood next to Cali. She smelled of cold, fresh air and She emanated a happy energy. Her freckles seemed to twinkle on her face like stars in the sky.

"Can I sit with you?" Veronica asked.

Sixth graders typically didn't welcome younger kids to share their seats, but Veronica had just arrived on the bus by parachute through the roof hatch. She could do anything she wanted. Cali scooted over and Veronica slid in beside her. Her feet didn't reach the floor. She swung her legs happily as she studied Cali. Uncomfortable, Cali turned her head to stare out the window.

Undeterred, Veronica asked, "Why did you get on this bus?"

Cali gave an impatient sigh. The questions just kept coming. "The bus stopped for me and I got on. If I had known there was another bus maybe I would have waited for it."

"*Phshhaw*, the other bus," Veronica said, waving her hand dismissively. "You didn't *have* to get on this bus," she said. Without waiting for an answer she turned to Mr. Fennelmyer. "She didn't *have* to get on this bus, right, Mr. Fennelmyer?"

"Of course not. Nobody rides Bus 13 unless they choose to. I watched her choose."

"But, will she stay?"

"Why are you asking me that?" Mr. Fennelmyer asked. "You know I've been wrong before. It's up to Cali."

"You were wrong about Fenton," Veronica said, a pout forming on her lips.

"I've already admitted I was wrong. Give me a break." Mr. Fennelmyer sounded hurt.

"I still have a choice to ride the other bus?" Cali asked.

Veronica looked at Cali sharply. Her expression said, *Why would you even ask that?* Her words were resentful, but surprisingly calm. "You could still choose to ride the other bus."

"I can? When?"

"When? What do you mean *when*? Whenever," Veronica said, huffily. "But if you choose to ride the other bus you'll never ride Bus 13 again, right, Mr. Fennelmyer?"

Mr. Fennelmyer glanced over his shoulder. "You talk too much," he said.

"I know," Veronica said, sulkily. "We're not supposed to tell you all this."

Mr. Fennelmyer glanced back and rolled his eyes. "There you go again."

Cali was trying to understand. "I won't be allowed back on this bus if I choose to ride the other bus?" That sounded mean and unfair.

"You won't even see this bus in the mornings again if you choose the normal bus."

"Veronica!" Mr. Fennelmyer warned.

"Sorry," she said, wiping her nose with her hand. In a small voice she added, "I just want Cali to stay."

It was silly, yet Cali was touched. "Why do you say that?"

Veronica looked up and studied Cali's face. She studied it so long that Cali shifted uncomfortably. "There's something different about you," Veronica finally said.

"Different? About me?" Cali almost laughed. "I'd say I'm the most boring person aboard this bus. I'm the muggle among the wizards. I'm the gray crayon among all the bright colors. I'm the eggshell in the scrambled eggs." Her parents sometimes played a game called Metaphor Wars at dinner. It really helped at times like these. She would have gone on, but Veronica interrupted.

"Your different is *different* from the way the kids on this bus are different," Veronica said, passionately.

Cali was speechless for a moment. When she found her voice she stuttered. "You . . . you've looked at me once and you know all this?"

"I *know*," Veronica said.

"Oh, she knows," Mr. Fennelmyer confirmed, as he turned onto a lonely road next to a field where sheep and llamas nibbled on mostly barren ground.

Veronica stared at her intensely with those clear green eyes. Cali covered her face with her hands. When she lowered her hands she was met with green eyes and freckles. Veronica was on her knees on the seat and had put her face right in front of Cali's.

"You're going to stay, and you're going to like it! Okay?" Veronica said. She put a hand on each side of Cali's face so that she couldn't look away. She stared into Cali's eyes several seconds longer, as if she could convince Cali by sheer will.

Veronica's eyes were like a kaleidoscope of broken green glass with edges of faded yellow. Looking into them brought back the tingling, magic she felt when the bus doors opened to her this morning. She had wanted nothing more than to ride Bus 13. She hadn't known the magic included gas and pipes and parachutes. What was her place among all this?

"I don't know," Cali said, lowering her eyes and looking at her hands. "I just don't know."

"Oh, good gravy!" Veronica sniffed and plopped back down on the seat next to Cali.

Chapter 7 – Fog On a Clear Day

"Watch the language, Ronni," Mr. Fennelmyer said.

"Good gravy?"

"I like gravy," he said. "No reason to swear by it."

"Sorry, but I can't help it." She wiped her eyes. "Why won't she stay with us?" She looked at Cali as she asked this question.

Cali saw tear smears on Veronica's hands. Guilt made her angry. Why did Veronica care whether or not she rode the bus?

When you are stuck, answer a question with a question, her father said.

"How old are you?" asked Cali.

"Ten."

It worked, she thought. *I have to remember to thank my dad.*

"And your parents let you skydive?"

"For a long time they didn't, and then at first I had to be strapped to one of them." She sounded offended by the memory.

"Strapped to one of them?"

"You know, tandem."

Cali gave her a blank look.

"I was harnessed with my Mom for the first five jumps. She had full control. It's like they thought I would forget to deploy my chute or something. Like *I* want to turn into a crater in the ground." Veronica rolled her eyes at her parents' impertinence.

"Why do you parachute to the bus?" Cali was pleased redirection had worked. She was sincerely interested now.

"How else am I supposed to catch the bus?"

"Couldn't they drive you to the bus stops?"

"There's no roads. We live off the grid." Veronica said this proudly.

Cali had heard of people living off grid, with no electricity or utilities. These people's children were usually home schooled.

"Why don't your parents teach you at home?"

Veronica shrugged. "They both work. Mom teaches biology at the University of Utah and Dad is a travel agent."

"But they live off grid," said Cali.

"That doesn't mean they don't like their jobs," pointed out Veronica. "The airplane lets them have it both ways. Now that I jump, they don't have to land."

Cali wondered at Veronica. Most kids were excited to get a driver's license. That would be anticlimactic for her.

Veronica raised her hand and gently rubbed the side of her face. She probed with her fingers and flinched.

"Are you okay?" Cali asked.

"I bumped my head on the way back up," Veronica said with a dismissive grin.

"I am so sorry," Mr. Fennelmyer apologized from the driver's seat. "I should have never let you talk me into trying to catch you through the hatch."

"You're an adult. You're supposed to know better," Veronica said, with a mischievous smile. To Cali she whispered, "It took me a month to talk him into trying."

"Let me see," Cali said.

Veronica turned her head so Cali could see the other side.

"Oh, you're going to have a shiner," Cali said, noting the swelling underneath and to the side of her eye.

"A shiner?"

"A black eye," Cali explained. "My dad calls them shiners."

"Why?"

"I guess because they swell up and get black and shiny."

"What does your dad do?" Veronica asked, as if what he did would explain why he called black eyes shiners.

"He's a lawyer."

"'A shiner' doesn't sound very lawyer-like."

"What should he say, then?"

"*Humongous blackus eyeicus*. That's Latin, right? And Lawyers speak Latin."

Cali laughed, not sure if she was laughing at Veronica's naiveté or her cleverness.

"That's not Latin, it only sounds like it" Cali said. "Besides, Dad doesn't speak Latin. He just knows some Latin law phrases."

Cali thought a moment and laughed again.

"What's so funny?" Veronica asked.

"Your *blackus eyeicus* made me think of something my dad says and tries to pass off as Latin. I don't know if I should tell you."

"You have to tell me now."

"Why?"

Mr. Fennelmyer spoke up. "Unwritten law. If a person ever says out loud 'I don't know if I should tell you' they have to tell you."

That almost made sense to Cali.

"Okay, whenever I beat him at Monopoly, or Metaphor Wars, or some other game, he calls me *Smarticus Assicus*."

Cali heard a giggle and a snort from behind. She looked back to see Felicia and Shelley leaning into the aisle listening in.

It took Veronica longer to get it. Her mouth dropped open and she said, "Ohhh."

Mr. Fennelmyer looked at her in his mirror and raised a disapproving eyebrow.

"You asked me to tell you," Cali said, defensively.

"You don't have to do everything I say," said Mr. Fennelmyer. After a short pause he recanted, "No, that's wrong. Yes, you do have to do everything I say. I'll just have to be more careful."

A shadow passed by the window. Veronica's eyes grew large as she looked out the window over Cali's shoulder.

"Oh, no!" she said.

Cali turned and looked out the window. She didn't see anything except the mountains on the other side of the valley and the clear sky above.

"What?" she asked. Then she saw. Another shadow passed by the window. It looked like a long wisp of gray smoke.

"Whose house is next?" Veronica asked.

"The Frankels'," Mr. Fennelmyer said.

"Oh, no," Veronica said, more dramatically this time. "It's the second time this month."

"This *is* odd," said Mr. Fennelmyer.

"It's the *Frankels*," called out Jimmy. "They live for this stuff." He pulled a harmonica out of his pocket and started playing The Twilight Zone theme music.

"Nobody lives for this stuff." Ice hung from Shelley's words. She leaned forward and glared at Jimmy over the back of his seat. Her eyes dead serious.

Jimmy's tune stopped mid-note. He tried to meet her stare, but he only lasted a moment. "I stand corrected," he said. He put his harmonica back to his lips and started playing again, but more softly than before.

"What is it?" asked Cali.

Veronica leaned out into the aisle and pointed out the windshield. Cali had to stand to see over the safety partition.

A large patch of ground fog covered the road ahead of them. It spread out a mile or so to either side and then tapered off suddenly. The rest of the valley was completely clear.

"Cool," said Cali. Even at eleven, she still took pleasure in running through the fog on rare occasions. She loved the ghostlike quality the fog gave to the everyday things around her. They were driving right through this patch of fog.

It was two or three full seconds before she felt Veronica's gaze. It was full of confusion and fear.

"What? I love the fog," Cali said.

"It's her first time," Brac said from right behind her.

Cali turned to see that Bric, Brac, and Freddy had moved up to the front. Marty and Marcus were on their way up the aisle lugging their chemical laboratory lunchboxes with them. All of them focused on the fog.

"She doesn't know," Freddy said.

"Know what?" Cali asked. *It's just fog, right?* They were creeping her out for the third or fourth time. She looked at Mr. Fennelmyer expecting him to tell them to knock off the joking. He, too, was focused on the fog. The bus was slowing down.

They hit the wall of fog. The promise of a beautiful day disappeared as if somebody flicked a switch. It was replaced by a sea of dark gray nothing. Cali wouldn't have guessed the fog was so thick. She could no longer see the barbed wire fence that was just three feet off the narrow road. She couldn't even see the road immediately in front of the bus. She was in a yellow blimp floating through a dark cloud high in the sky.

"Do you see any?" Bric said.

"Nothing," Marcus answered from the seat behind his.

"Shouldn't you be making a b-beacon?" Jimmy said with a slight stutter.

"I'm on it," Marcus said.

Cali heard him open his lunchbox and saw a soft green glow reflect off the ceiling over him.

What is going on?

She wanted to ask out loud, but the atmosphere on the bus had gotten so serious she was afraid to disturb it.

She heard movement behind her. Shelley was squeezing past Felicia into the aisle. In the dimming light her eyes shone a more intense blue than they had earlier.

Mr. Fennelmyer looked in his mirror. "Take a seat, Shelley. We didn't need you last time. We're not going to need you today, either."

The difference between truth and lies is sometimes imperceptible, Cali's mother said. Mr. Fennelmyer was lying about not needing Shelley today. Cali didn't even know what he meant, but she knew he didn't believe his own words. Cali understood that. Mr. Fennelmyer was trying to make something true by hoping.

What is it they're all afraid of? She desperately wanted to know.

Felicia hurried forward and gently took Shelley's arm. She coaxed her into the seat across from Cali's and slid in next to her.

Mr. Fennelmyer suddenly hit the brakes. "Well, I never," he said, in exasperation and fear.

Cali was thrown against the seat in front of her. She scrambled up to see why they had braked. She was just in time to see the last of several large dogs flash through the headlights. They disappeared into the fog at the side of the bus. At least that is what she thought she saw. The truth was that she hadn't really seen them. She had the *impression* that they were there. It was as if the fog itself had momentarily taken the shape of a pack of dogs and then melted back into fog again.

"Were those—" Cali began.

"Wolves," Veronica finished. "I hate the wolves." She grabbed Cali's arm and tried to hide her head behind it.

"Did you hit any of them?" Cali asked.

"Ha," Mr. Fennelmyer said. "I don't think you *can* hit them. They just surprised me is all. They've never run across in front of me like that before."

"They're up to something," Bric said. "The Frankels better be on the ball this morning."

"We're still a couple of miles away from the Frankels," said Mr. Fennelmyer, "and they were running the wrong direction. I bet we've seen the last of them today."

He's doing it again, thought Cali. *He's hoping for a truth.*

They drove on, slowly. The kids all kept watch out the windows. Cali found herself keeping watch, too. She didn't understand why. Goosebumps spread from her spine to her arms. She was absolutely certain that she didn't want to ride this bus. She didn't want to get off here, though. Definitely not here.

"You know," Freddy said, "this is the only bad part of riding Bus 13."

He sounded genuinely spooked. 'Spooked' is contagious. Cali grew even more anxious.

School buses are safe, her father said when she asked why there were no seatbelts. *Schools are so afraid of lawsuits that they actually stumble over all the safety regulations they create. Just ask a bus driver to list all the regulations he has to follow, and then be prepared to sit for an hour while he tells you.*

Cali wanted to ask Mr. Fennelmyer, right then, to list all the safety regulations. She would have, too, if he wasn't so busy watching for ghostly wolves in mysterious fog. Cali realized, in that instant, that the safety regulations her father talked about did not apply to Bus 13. Bus 13 was dangerous. Veronica's swelling eye attested to that.

"If you don't like this, then why do you keep riding Bus 13?" Cali asked.

"When we are in the fog I can never remember why," Freddy said. "I'll have to tell you later."

When you're not scared, thought Cali.

Cali heard a low growl. Shelley was looking past Cali out the window. Her eyes were bright blue.

"I can't see them, but Shelley says they're over there," Brac said, peering hard through the window behind Cali's.

Veronica leaned in to Cali and whispered, "These fogs are especially hard on Shelley."

"Why?' Cali whispered back.

Veronica glanced across the aisle. "Can't you tell?"

"Tell what?" Cali asked. The fact that Shelley was strange?

"That the wolves got her once," Veronica whispered, giving Cali the 'duh' look.

"The wolves got her?" Cali echoed. She looked across the aisle at the girl growling there. "She wasn't always like this?"

"Oh, no. She used to be kind of loud and obnoxious."

"This is what being 'got' by the wolves does to you?" Cali asked.

Veronica shrugged. "Nobody's been got like her before. It was two days before she came back, and she was like this." Veronica leaned in and whispered even lower, "I kind of like her better now."

Glancing over at Shelley, Cali expected the growl to become a bark at any moment.

During all this growling and suspense Felicia sat, calmer than the rest. As Shelley's growling grew louder, Felicia reached into her coat and pulled out a large piece of beef jerky. With a lot of pulling and twisting she bit a piece off the end. Cali's mouth watered. She loved jerky.

I wish she would have offered me that instead of the muffin earlier.

"Mmmm," Felicia said, while chomping away.

"Who's eating jerky?" Marty said, from two seats back. He rose a little in his seat to see, causing bottles to rattle against each other.

"Watch it," Marcus said. "That stuff stains. You know what Mr. Fennelmyer will say."

"But someone's eating jerky."

"It's Felicia," said Bric.

"She wouldn't do that in front of us," said Freddy. He sounded disappointed.

"Shhhh," said Brac. "She's doing her thing."

Shelley's nose twitched. She had been so focused on the wolves that the scent of the jerky hadn't penetrated right away. Her eyes dimmed a little as she turned and looked at Felicia.

"Want some?" Felicia asked, still chomping. She held out the jerky.

Shelley snatched it and immediately began gnawing away.

Shelley's rude action didn't bother Felicia at all.

Felicia read the look on Cali's face. "Oh, I brought it just for Shelley," she said. "It's her comfort food."

"It makes me feel better too," said Marcus, a little sadly.

Felicia flashed him an apologetic smile. "That's all I have." Watching Shelley hungrily tearing off another bite, she added, "And I wouldn't try to take it from her just now."

With Shelley's growling temporarily gone, the bus quieted. Eventually Mr. Fennelmyer spoke.

"It's thinning," he said. "And there's the Frankels' house. No sign of the wolves. I told you it would be fine."

CHAPTER 8 – WOLVES

Cali could just make out a large, brick house sitting off the road with a circular drive. Lights shone through the multi-paned living room window softly illuminating the grey mist.

"At least they're not waiting out here as usual," said Marty.

"They may be adventurous, but they're not stupid," answered Brac.

"Well, they don't like Bach," Jimmy said, considering Brac's statement.

"Come on, Frankels," cheered Felicia expectantly as she peered toward the house.

As if that were their cue, the front door opened spilling out more light. Three hazy figures emerged, one after the other, coming toward the bus at a run.

"That's right," muttered Mr. Fennelmyer, "fleet of foot in the fog."

They were halfway to the bus when Freddy cried out, "They're here!"

A collective cry sounded in the bus. Cali looked in the direction Freddy was pointing. Red eyes gleamed out of the murk; black noses and claws floated up and down as the wolves loped toward the bus. Mist swirled where their bodies should have been. Cali wasn't sure a person could actually touch the wolves any more than touch the fog. Their presence was frightening nonetheless.

"Ha! The wolves are too late," yelled Bric.

"Don't jinx the kids," snapped Mr. Fennelmyer.

The three children were swiftly closing on the bus.

Cali held her breath as she looked back and forth from running children to burning eyes and leaping claws. She cried out with the others when the smallest child, tailing behind, dropped his bag of marbles on the driveway. The marbles spilled and rolled in every direction.

"I don't believe it," said Bric.

"Just like a first grader," added Brac.

"What's he thinking? It's not even marble season," said Freddy.

The first two figures leaped through the bus door and ran up the steps.

"Ha ha! Beat them again," the second figure said, turning up the aisle behind her brother. She started to say more, but was cut off.

"Just leave them!" Mr. Fennelmyer yelled.

Brother and sister, both dressed in coonskin caps and leather clothes like Daniel Boone, looked out a window. Their brother was grabbing at the marbles on the ground.

"Warren!" the girl cried.

Warren didn't look up until the wolves leapt upon him.

Cali watched in horror as the eyes, the claws, and the occasional shape of a tail enveloped the boy. Totally helpless she watched as Warren, belly down, reached toward the bus as he was dragged off into the fog.

The bus went silent as everyone stared at where Warren had been. Devon and Marissa rushed for the door. Mr. Fennelmyer flipped the switch. The doors hissed shut in their faces.

"Open the door," yelled Marissa. Devon turned and glared at Mr. Fennelmyer.

"Go to your seats," Mr. Fennelmyer said.

"We aren't going to just let the wolves have my brother." Marissa's brown eyes sparked as she spoke. Cali pictured Marissa throwing hatchets at trees after school. Her brother, quieter, stood beside her in support.

"We aren't going to leave him," said Mr. Fennelmyer. "But if I let you two go after him you know as well as I do that the wolves will end up with three children instead of one."

"I *don't* know that," Marissa said, defiantly. She tried to stare Mr. Fennelmyer down, but lost. Mr. Fennelmyer met her eyes with a gentle, steady gaze until Marissa's eyes filled with tears. "Okay," she said, "but hurry."

As distraught as she was, Marissa stared at Cali through her tears as she walked by.

"Shelley!" Mr. Fennelmyer barked.

Shelley leaped up next to the driver's seat.

"You and I have talked about this possible situation since—" he hesitated, "your experience. Do you still think you can do it?"

Shelley, in her low, gravelly voice, answered without hesitation. "I can do it."

"I know you can, too," Mr. Fennelmyer said.

Cali heard a twinge of fear in his voice. *He's doing that wishful lying again.*

Mr. Fennelmyer flipped the switch and the doors clunked open.

"But I'll need help," Shelley added.

She grabbed Cali's hand hard and pulled her out of her seat, down the stairs, and out the door.

"Shelley! No!" yelled Mr. Fennelmyer.

Cali found herself being pulled through fog so dense she could barely make out the ground beneath her feet. Shelley moved so quickly Cali could barely remain upright.

When they finally stopped they were standing in the tall, dry weeds of a field.

"What are you doing?" Cali asked in a shaky, breathless voice. She was terrified and near tears. The wolves were out here. She expected to see red eyes and black claws approaching at any moment.

"It's okay," Shelley said. The glow of her eyes created a halo effect around her face.

"Okay?" Cali couldn't believe her ears. "What's okay? You saw what the wolves did to Warren. They're going to do it to me, too."

"They didn't do anything to Warren except take him away," Shelley said. She stepped close to Cali. Cali almost stepped back until she realized she could now actually see Shelley's face through the fog. "Remember?"

On the bus Shelley looked anxious, awkward—like she didn't feel at home. The face in front of her now was calm and full of confidence. Her glowing eyes lost their squintiness. They were bright and eager.

Remember? Cali remembered the swirling mist, the fiery eyes, and the claws. They were horrible. Then she remembered Warren being pulled off into the fog on his belly, his eyes wide with fear and his hand reaching toward them for help. He had looked frightened, but not hurt.

"He was reaching toward us, frightened," Cali said.

"Well, the wolves are a little scary, and it's not like he wanted to go with them." Had Shelley chuckled? The sound she made was low and growly. It certainly could have been a chuckle.

"That's the problem," Shelley went on. "We have to find him before they talk him into staying." She turned and, with a lurch, began pulling Cali through the fog again.

"You are hurting my hand," Cali said, half whispering, half yelling.

"Sorry," said Shelley, stepping back into Cali's space. "I didn't want you to run back to the bus."

"I don't even know where the bus is."

"Oh, right." There was that low, growly chuckle again.

"My hand?" Cali said. Shelley still clung to it.

"Sorry," Shelley said, letting go.

Cali rubbed her hand wishing she knew which way the bus was.

"What did you mean 'We have to find him before they talk him into staying?'" Cali asked.

"They're *very* persuasive," Shelley said.

"The wolves?" Cali had to make sure they were talking about the same thing. "They can talk?"

"Not exactly, but close enough," Shelley said.

"I don't understand." Her voice wavered.

A wolf howled in the fog. Its eerie, high-pitched tone trailed off slowly.

"They're talking to him now," Shelley said, looking toward the sound. "We need to hurry."

"Drag me if you must, but I'm not moving my feet until you explain." Even as she spoke, Cali moved closer and took Shelley's arm. The call of the wolf had her trembling.

Shelley looked at Cali, then toward the sound of the howl. "The wolves," she began. She spoke so quietly that Cali had to move even closer to hear. "They lived here for a thousand years hunting elk and deer. When the Indians came the wolves made friends with them and shared the land and game. The Indians respected the wolves, and the wolves the Indians. Then white people came. They hated the wolves. They said it was because they ate their cattle and sheep, but really they were just afraid. They hunted the wolves until they were nearly exterminated. As the wolves went, so did the Indians.

"The leader of the last wolf pack met with the last great Indian medicine man and asked for a blessing. The medicine man spent ten days dancing and singing to the Great Spirit on behalf of the wolves. The Great Spirit separated the wolves from the white man's world so the white man could no longer harm them.

"This last pack of wolves was able to run free and live with the Indians, all the while being undetected by the white man. Eventually the medicine man died. The last Indians left and the wolves became lonely. They started to seek out human companions to live with them and tell them stories. They push against the edge of their world into the white man's world—our world—fog forms. We see the wolves in it."

Shelley paused, turning her face to Cali. "They say they just want a friend."

In her mind Cali saw the wolves running free across the land. She saw a girl running with them, her hair flying in the wind, her arms and legs flashing in the sun. Her hands slipped from Shelley's arm and the vision ended.

Cali came back to herself. "Shelley, how do you know all this?"

"One morning the wolves got me." Shelley's voice grew wistful. "They told me if I stayed I could run free as the wind with them, forever. They made me feel so welcome, so needed. They said I would have powers like theirs if I stayed.

"From the first moment I could run as fast on two legs as they could on four. They said that had never happened before and that one day I would be their queen. I wanted that more than anything. I thought I would never want to leave them. We ran and howled. At night they laid their bodies against me and kept me warm."

Shelley stopped, lost in memory. She swallowed noisily before going on. "Everything was fine until I got hungry." She looked at Cali. "You still get hungry there."

Cali nodded.

"So on my second day they hunted. I ran with them, led the way, and helped them force a doe into a tangle of scrub oak. I stopped when they attacked the doe. I didn't know it would be like that." Shelley paused, a haunted look in her eyes.

"One of the wolves, the leader, told me that all I had to do was lick one drop of blood and I would be like them forever. Then the doe would taste better than the greatest feast I ever had. That's how it had been for her."

"Her?" Cali asked. "The leader was female?"

"Not just female; she had been a girl like me. I looked into her eyes then and saw a face reflected there. It wasn't mine.

"*Sheila.* Her name came to me like a whisper. I realized what it would mean to become a wolf forever. I could never go home. Sheila saw what I was thinking and got angry. She told me I was changing already. I would never be the same again.

"She was telling the truth. I could feel the difference in me. It was frightening and wonderful. I almost changed my mind to stay, but Mr. Fennelmyer and Bus 13 were looking for me. I heard the bus horn and Mr. Fennelmyer calling from the edge of the other world. He gave me courage and I ran."

"Did the wolves try to stop you?" Cali asked.

"Only Sheila. The rest stayed and gorged on the doe. To Sheila I was more important than eating. I don't know why. I beat her to the bus. She howled in anger when I got on. It was sad and frightening."

"Oh, Shelley," Cali said, feeling sad and not knowing why.

"I've never told anyone that before," Shelley said.

Her eyes met Cali's just for a moment. "We have to rescue Warren."

She turned and disappeared into the fog.

CHAPTER 9 – HERE DOGGY, DOGGY

Cali panicked when Shelley disappeared. She ran a few steps forward. Not being able to see her feet on the ground made her feel dizzy.

"Shelley!" Her call wasn't much above a whisper. She was afraid Shelley wouldn't hear her; she was afraid the wolves would.

Shelley suddenly appeared at her side. "You have to stay with me or you'll get lost."

"How am I supposed to stay with you when you disappear in one step?" Cali answered, angrily.

"I keep forgetting," Shelley said, palming her forehead. She eyed Cali for a moment and then said, "Take off your scarf."

Cali had added on the scarf that morning as an afterthought.

It brings out the gold highlights in your eyes, her mother said.

Cali unwrapped the wrinkled cotton fabric from around her neck and handed it to Shelley.

Shelley lifted her dress to get to the top of the jeans she wore underneath. She took one end of the scarf and pushed it through the belt loop on the side of her jeans and tied a simple knot. "You hang on to the other end," she said. "Don't let go."

"Wait a minute," Cali said. "What did you mean when you said, 'I keep forgetting?'"

"What?" said Shelley. "Oh. I keep forgetting that you can't see in the fog."

"And you can?" Cali asked.

"Yes," Shelly said. She turned, and was off

I suppose that must be the upside of glowing eyes, Cali thought as she was jerked into motion.

They ran at a fast pace. Cali stumbled over clumps of weeds, sagebrush, and uneven ground until she fell on her face. Cali, who held on to the scarf with obsessed determination, was dragged for three feet.

"We're here," she said, kneeling beside Cali. She didn't ask why Cali was face down on the ground.

"Quit your worrying. I'll be fine," Cali said, sarcastically.

"Shhhh, they'll hear you."

Cali sat up and brushed herself off. "Where are they?" she whispered.

"Right over there." Shelley pointed.

Cali might as well have had her nose against a white wall—she couldn't see a thing. She could feel Shelley's tenseness. The butterflies in her stomach started fluttering. "If you can see them how come they can't see us?"

"Because they aren't looking for us," Shelley said in a low voice. "We're sitting in the blurry space between their world and our world and they just aren't paying attention. They got Warren and that's all they care about."

Shelley knelt there studying the wolves through the fog. Cali couldn't get over the difference between the Shelley here and the Shelley on the bus. Here she was focused, confident, and articulate. Cali felt safe in her presence in spite of the danger from the wolves. Cali felt completely useless out here. *Why did she bring me with her?*

"Do you have a plan?" Cali whispered.

Shelley appeared to think, then said, "I thought we would just walk out there calling 'Good doggy.' Then we could scratch them behind the ears and rub their tummies. After that they'll be so relaxed they will let Warren go."

Cali's mouth dropped open.

Shelley looked at Cali, grinning. "Just kidding." She turned serious as she went on. "I'm going to run out there and distract the wolves.

I'm pretty sure they'll follow me. When they do, you run out and grab Warren. He's small so you just pick him up and carry him back to the bus. Any questions?"

Any Questions? Yes, she had questions. The first was *How can I grab him if I can't see him?* Next was, *How am I supposed to find the school bus?* Then, *What if they catch you?* And finally, *What if they catch me?*

Shelley sprinted away into the fog.

Cali sat in shock.

"Shelley!" she whispered hoarsely. "*Shelley?*" Her heart raced and she felt tears of fear in her throat.

Just then Shelley's voice, sounding far away, floated through the fog. "Cali, *now!*"

The urgency in the voice brought Cali to her feet in spite of her fear. With her hands held out in front of her she stumbled forward. Her third step brought her abruptly into dazzling sunlight.

"Oh," she stopped, squinting. She was in a different world indeed. A meadow of wild flowers stretched out before her. Woods of quaking aspens started mixing with pines higher up on the surrounding hills. Behind the hills in the distance, dark, rocky peaks jutted into the sky with ribbons of snow in shadowy crevasses. The beauty of the scene momentarily stunned Cali. She forgot why she was there.

She saw the movement on the far side of the meadow—it was Shelley. She was running like the wind with a pack of wolves on her heels. The sight made Cali sick to her stomach. The wolves would catch her and— Cali couldn't bear to think about it.

Movement in the flowers caught her attention. She turned to run certain that it was a wolf that remained behind,. Looking over her shoulder she was relieved to see Warren stand up.

"Warren," she called, running to him.

Warren glanced at her and then stared in the direction Shelley and the wolves had run. He still had his raccoon hat on.

"Shelley knocked me down," he complained. "She did it on purpose, too."

Warren was about six years old, and skinny with blond hair poking out from under his coon cap. He looked cute in his leather Davey Crockett outfit.

"Come on," Cali said, grabbing his arm. "We have to go."

She turned toward the fog only to have Warren jerk his arm away.

"Where are *they* going?" he asked looking across the meadow.

Cali's fear made her speak sharply. "Shelley's distracting the wolves so we can escape. Come *on*."

She reached for his arm, but he hopped out of range.

"Look at her run," Warren said, admiration in his voice.

Shelley came out of the trees on the top of a ridge. The wolves were actually snapping at her heels. If she stumbled or slowed even for an instant they would be on her.

Oh, Shelley, run, she thought. Where was Mr. Fennelmyer? How could he be allowing this?

Warren was right; she did run like wind moving through tall grass. Shelley had just run across the meadow, through the woods, and up a steep hill. The wolves should have caught her long before this. Was Shelley running for her life, or was she just teasing the wolves?

Cali watched Shelley disappear over the top of the ridge. Warren, caught up in the sight of the chase, raised his head and howled. His high, six-year-old howl carried in the mountain air. Too late Cali realized the danger and slapped her hand over his mouth.

To her horror the largest of the wolves appeared again looking down from the top of the ridge. The sight of the wolf took her breath away, not for fear, but for beauty. Its white body was silhouetted by the dark peaks behind it. It held its large head high with red eyes glowing. It was magnificent. Piercing eyes fell upon her and Warren reminding Cali of the danger. Her heart skipped two beats when she saw the wolf start down this side of the ridge—it was coming back for them.

"We have to go, *now!*" Cali said.

Warren slipped from her grasp again.

"They said I could run with them," he yelled. "Why does Shelley get to if I can't?" He lurched away from her and started toward the woods, his little legs pumping fast.

In desperation, Cali leaped forward and tackled Warren. She landed on him harder than she meant. She felt the breath go out of him. She wanted to apologize, to check if he was okay, but in the woods just across the meadow the wolf was coming for them.

Cali put her arms around Warren's chest and picked him up. She ignored the look of pain on his face as he struggled for breath. He was heavier than he looked. Feeling incredibly slow, she half ran, half stumbled for the wall of fog. Just before she entered the fog she glanced over her shoulder. The wolf burst from the woods, its red eyes focused on them.

The eyes had a powerful effect on her. Her legs went weak and she almost sunk to her knees. Then she heard a muffled voice through the fog.

"Cali! Shelley! We're over here. We're over here!"

She recognized the voices. There was Mr. Fennelmyer, Veronica, Bric and Brac—they were still there. As heartening as it was to hear their voices it was the organ music that gave her strength. For some inane reason Jimmy was playing "On Top of Old Smokey." Out of her mind with fear she almost laughed as she remembered her father singing his silly words. He had learned the tune in Boy Scouts.

On top of spaghetti, all covered with cheese,

I lost my poor meatball, when somebody sneezed.

Cali rearranged her grip on Warren and threw him over her shoulder.

It rolled off the table, and onto the floor.

And then my poor meatball, rolled right out the door.

With his weight now balanced she ran into the fog. The meadow disappeared replaced with a dim, eternal gray nothingness.

It rolled into the garden, and under a bush.

And then my poor meatball, was nothing but mush.

Warren bounced on her shoulder. Unable to see where she was going, Cali moved more at a trot than a run. Behind her the wolf would be closing fast. She had no idea how far away the bus was. The music, along with the memory of her father's voice in her head, kept her steady.

That mush was as tasty, as tasty could be.

And then my poor meatball, grew into a tree.

The sound of the music drifted to her left, so she adjusted her course.

"My hat!" Warren gasped. "My hat fell off."

"Sorry, kid," Cali said. "Stopping for your marbles got us in this position in the first place. We're not stopping for your hat."

He started squirming and kicking so hard Cali could hardly hold on to him. Warren fell off her shoulder, but she caught him on the way down. She held him around the waist up on her hip and staggered forward. Finally, he quit struggling. That would have been a relief, except he started crying instead. Somewhere amid her frustration and fear, Cali actually felt bad for him.

"I'll buy you another one, okay?" she said, wondering where in the world a person buys coonskin hats. To her surprise, Warren calmed down. It was then that the music stopped. Her heart sank. She felt abandoned. Without the music every direction looked the same.

"Help!" she yelled.

She was so winded that it was more of a gasp than a yell. She thought she heard voices, but nobody was calling to her anymore. "Where's the bus?" she croaked. There was no answer. She stumbled forward with Warren held backwards on her hip not knowing if she was getting nearer to the bus, or farther away.

Cali was making only slow progress now. She was sure the wolf was going to leap on them any instant. She chanced a glance over her shoulder. Red eyes came bounding through the fog. The bus was close, but where? Her legs kept moving even though she didn't feel connected to them anymore. In terror she braced for the impact of the wolf on her back.

It never came.

The wolf leaped past and whirled around to face them. In the meadow the wolf had looked solid. In the fog it was ghostly. The wolf's eyes were blazing. Its body was a tight, swirling mass of vapor suggesting legs, body, and tail. The head seemed solid enough.

Cali's legs stopped moving. She closed her eyes as Warren slipped off her shoulder and fell to the ground.

I failed, she thought. *I'm sorry, Shelley.*

Beside her she heard Warren getting to his feet.

"Sheila," he said. There was a tremor in his voice. "Is that my hat?"

Cali opened her eyes. The wolf held Warren's coonskin hat in its jaws. Did Warren just call the wolf *Sheila?*

Although the wolf's mouth didn't move Cali heard an accusing voice—it seemed to whisper from the fog itself. *You said you'd run with us, Warren.*

Somewhere in the whispering, growling voice Cali sensed the tones of a human girl.

"I . . . I wanted to," Warren stammered, "but someone knocked me down and then you ran away so fast."

Shelley! The word came out a snarl. The fiery eyes narrowed.

Warren leaned in to Cali and took her hand. If he hadn't been afraid of the wolves before, he was now.

With a flick of her head the wolf sent the coonskin cap flying into the fog behind Cali and Warren.

You can still come, the voice said, gently this time. Her eyes had softened with the tone of her voice. *Go get your hat and come with me now.*

Warren hesitated. Was he thinking about going with the wolves, or was he just thinking about his hat? She put her arm around him, ready to grab him if she needed to.

"I don't want to anymore," Warren said, in a small, frightened voice.

Come with me! It was a command this time. The wolf's upper lip pulled back revealing deadly fangs. The fog seemed to swirl with her snarl. Warren threw his arms around Cali's waist and hid his face against her. Cali pulled him even closer for what little good it would do against the wolf.

Betrayal! The voice growled in a rumble so low that Cali didn't think Jimmy's pipe organ could reach it. *Shelley betrayed me and now you. I want to go home. Someone must stay so that I can go.*

Cali, frozen in fear, couldn't even blink. The wolf looked directly into her eyes. Underneath the blazing red Cali became aware of a softer color—yellow. It was hard to see in the red of rage, but it was there, a warm yellow like a living room light shining through the window on a cold January night.

Please, said the voice, softer, more human and girlish.

Can a wolf cry? Cali didn't think so, but she was sure she heard tears in that one word.

There was a flash and then a brilliant green light illuminated the fog. Startled, the wolf yelped and leaped into the fog, disappearing. Cali squinted her eyes in the direction where the light was strongest. Behind the source of the light she saw the shadowy outline of the bus. She could even see the shapes of heads and torsos in the windows.

Grabbing Warren's arm she pulled him toward he bus. The fog thinned as they neared. The children, faces framed by windows, cheered when they saw Cali and Warren.

"Oh, Cali." Veronica's voice rose above the others. She sounded near tears

"Cali! Cali!" chanted Bric, Brac, and Freddy.

Marty and Marcus appeared to be in the middle of mixing something. They waved beakers and test tubes as they cheered. Marissa and Devon were at the front windows calling Warren's name. Mr. Fennelmyer stood in the doorway motioning them to hurry. As soon as she reached the door they lifted Warren into Mr. Fennelmyer's arms and he hauled Warren up the steps to safety.

Before Cali could mount the first step the cheering stopped. The silence was unnerving. Cali turned slowly to see Sheila not three feet from her. She was more wolf than fog now. Her entire form was solid. She was white as snow, except for the eyes, nose, and claws. Her head stood as high as Cali's chest. Sheila's eyes were different now, a duller red with warmer yellow where the pupils should be.

Cali knew she should be leaping into the safety of the bus. Sheila's gaze held her fast.

Please.

It was just one word, soft and pleading, in the thinning fog. Cali didn't know why, but it broke her heart. Her fingers slipped from the handrail and she stepped toward the wolf.

A hand grabbed her arm and pulled her into the bus. It was Mr. Fennelmyer. He said something, but it was lost in the most heartbreaking howl ever heard.

Mr. Fennelmyer flicked a switch and the doors shut in front of Cali. Was it to keep the wolf out, or to keep her in? She sat on the stairs feeling a sadness she didn't understand.

Sheila.

Another name brought her to her senses.

"Here comes Shelley," Felicia called, relieved.

Cali stumbled up the steps. Shelley came running full speed across the Frankels' lawn, the pack of wolves trailing behind. The wolves were actually farther behind now than when Cali saw them before. Their tongues lolled to the side and they looked worn out. She would beat the pack to the bus, but there was Sheila to deal with. She stood in front of the door in no mood to let the last human get away. The kids watched, breathless, wondering what Shelley was going to do.

Shelley saw Sheila, but didn't even slow down. As naturally as if it were her plan all along, she changed course at the last moment and leaped for an open window. With surprising agility she flew through the air like an arrow, arms first. Unfortunately she had chosen the window Freddy was occupying. Freddy, caught by surprise, didn't have time to move. Shelley slammed into him. They both tumbled into the aisle. The wolves didn't leap for the windows. Instead they circled restlessly around Sheila. She raised her head and howled. They joined her in an eerie, warbling chorus.

"Well, this is going to put us behind." Mr. Fennelmyer looked at his watch. He put the bus in gear and started up the road. The wolves, cutting their chorus short, ran beside the bus until the fog thinned and the sunlight grew brighter. The wolves simply evaporated. Cali stared back, wondering.

CHAPTER 10 – OF HEROES AND COWARDS

Freddy's loud complaints brought Cali out of her reverie.

"That is the third time today somebody landed on me. What do I look like, the floor?"

"You do seem to have a talent for softening the landing of others," Felicia said. "I'm certain Shelley and Veronica are grateful." She reached out and patted him on the head. Freddy, ignoring Shelley, who was still lying in a tangle on top of him, batted Felicia's hand away. Shelley licked his cheek.

"What the heck," yelled Freddy, trying to push Shelley off.

"You see," said Felicia, the only one to see Shelley's canine response, "she is grateful. But, Shelley, you need to remember you are a human girl, not a wolf."

Shelley and Freddy struggled to rise. Finally, they made it to their knees. Thinking about what Felicia said, Shelley remembered that humans kiss differently from dogs.

"No," Freddy said, reading the look in Shelley's eyes. "No, no, and no!"

Disappointed, Shelley squeezed between the two seats and got to her feet. Freddy did the same.

The kids broke into applause and cheered at the sight of Shelley. Marissa and Devon cheered the loudest. Warren pouted.

Cali didn't join in. She felt angry. They were cheering for the girl who had almost gotten her killed. It's fine if a girl with super wolf abilities wants to chance a rescue against supernatural wolves. Dragging along a girl too slow to make it to first base in a kickball game was unforgivable. Cali scowled at Shelley.

Smiling for the first time that day, Shelley turned toward Cali and slowly raised her arm the way a conductor does toward a soloist after a symphony.

"It was Cali," she said, her voice softer and less gravelly now. "She brought Warren back safely."

There was silence for a fraction of a second before celebratory noise erupted again, this time for Cali. Marty and Marcus quickly poured liquids into their jars and then slapped on the nozzle lids. The green liquid evaporated into gas, built up pressure, and then honked like air horns as it escaped through the nozzles. Bric and Brac tore up sheets of paper and threw the bits like confetti. Veronica danced on her seat and hugged Cali around the neck. Jimmy, whose pipes once again poked up from the seat in front of him, played a lively version of "For She's a Jolly Good Fellow." Mr. Fennelmyer sang the words with zest as he drove.

Cali couldn't stay angry. Only once before in her life had she experienced such public attention. That was for selling more boxes of chocolate than any other student at her elementary school in Salt Lake City. They didn't know it was because her mom and dad had bought fifty boxes. They were making up for forgetting to pick her up from a day camp at the Natural History Museum. Principal Bauer had called her up front during a school assembly and awarded her a McDonald's Gift Certificate. Kids had clapped for her only because they were expected to.

This was different. These kids were clapping and yelling with enthusiasm even though they didn't even know her. They met her eyes and smiled without embarrassment. She blushed and smiled in spite of herself.

"How did you do it?" called Bric over the applause. "It's not like I'm afraid of the wolves or anything, but I wouldn't go out in that fog for a million dollars cash—not even if Shelley dragged me out."

The bus quieted as the kids waited for her story.

"I . . . um." Cali struggled for words. Bric's choice of words made her feel awkward. Shelley *had* dragged her out of the bus.

Honesty is the best policy, said her mother.

"Um . . . I *was* drag—" she began.

"The thing is, Shelley needed her and she went," Mr. Fennelmyer said, interrupting.

"When I saw you running out of the fog with Warren over your shoulder I thought 'She's the boss!'" said Brac.

"And the way you stared down that wolf," said Marissa. She spoke almost reverently. "I thought you and Warren were both dead for sure."

"You . . . you saw that?" asked Cali. How could they see her when she couldn't see the bus?

Marissa nodded. "I would have fainted or peed my pants. You stood there as calm as could be."

Are they really talking about me? There was nothing heroic about her. She went to school, got decent grades, and minded her own business. She didn't participate in extra-curricular activities or get involved in anyone's causes. She didn't do any real good in the world at all.

I only looked calm because I was too afraid to move. All she had done was grab Warren and run for her life. *What would they think if they knew?*

History is made by the people who write it down, her Dad said. *Heroes are made by the people telling the story.*

Cali understood what her dad meant, now.

All the kids waited for her to say something. She was wondering what to say when she noticed that Shelley was holding something furry in her hand.

"Where did you get that?"

The other kids turned to see.

"Warren's hat," Shelley said, barely above a mumble. She turned and tossed it to Warren. Cali realized Shelley must have picked it up while running for the bus.

"Cool," said Warren. "Teeth holes." He pushed his fingers through the holes and wiggled them.

Cali stared at Shelley in wonder. "You took the time to pick up Warren's cap with a pack of wolves at your heels?"

"I didn't have to slow down. I just kind of swooped as I ran." She demonstrated a slow swoop in the aisle.

Everyone was looking at Shelley again. Cali felt relieved the attention was off her. She saw Shelley changing right before her eyes. The boldness, the focus, the confidence were seeping away. In moments she was just a quiet, shy girl with frizzy hair. Her bow was gone. It must have fallen off during the chase. She looked awkward wearing jeans under the yellow dress. Her eyes were still shining brightly.

"You should have seen her," Cali said, wanting to recreate the Shelley she had seen in the fog. "She distracted the wolves from Warren and me. We watched as she led the wolves away from us up over a ridge. They were snapping at her heels."

"She ran like the wind," added Warren, impressed by Shelley's awesomeness. Then he looked a Cali. "You run like my Old Granny."

Marissa slapped him on the back of the head knocking his hat off. "Don't be rude," she said. "Ol' Granny is his ancient swayback horse, not his grandma."

That didn't make Cali feel any better.

"Well, Cali 'bout broke me in two trotting with me over her shoulder."

"He didn't want to come," Cali explained, blushing, "and he's a lot heavier than he looks."

"It's 'cause I'm mostly muscle," he said, flexing a skinny bicep.

Once again she felt the discomfort of all eyes upon her. She looked over and saw Jimmy staring at her admiringly.

"While I was lost in the fog looking for the bus I could have sworn I heard music."

"Yes?" he said expectantly.

"It sounded a lot like 'On Top of Spaghetti.'"

Jimmy's look turned to pure adoration. "You have such class!" he said.

"Class? For recognizing a boy scout song?"

"Pure class," Jimmy said.

"I recognized it," said Bric.

"You thought it was "On Top of Old Smokey," said Jimmy.

"It's the same tune," said Freddy. "It's not like your organ was singing the words."

"Then how did Cali know which one I was playing?" Jimmy asked smugly.

The frustration on Bric's face made Cali laugh. Turning to Jimmy she asked, "But would Bach be pleased with your selection?"

"Oh, yes! If it helped save you, Bach would be pleased." Jimmy said this with complete certainty.

"Did you see the flash grenade?" asked Marcus. "We had to make it in a hurry and weren't sure it would work."

"It saved our lives," Cali said. "It scared the wolf out of our way so we could reach the bus door."

"Yes!" Marty and Marcus yelled at the same time. They gave each other high fives with their right hands, wiggled the fingers of their left hands together, and then hip bumped.

"Dorks," said Brac.

"Says the one who didn't help with the rescue," Marty said.

"Hey, I was yelling for them long before the music started or the flash grenade was ready. I was even hanging out the window where it was dangerous." He turned to Cali. "Did you hear me yelling?"

"I heard," Cali said.

Brac proudly stood taller.

"All right," Mr. Fennelmyer said, over the intercom. "Everybody in your seats. The celebration is over."

There was a collective groan.

"Hey," said Mr. Fennelmyer, "you know the safety rules."

"Somebody needs to tell the wolves about the safety rules," called out Devon.

"That's the truth," mumbled Cali.

The kids laughed. Mr. Fennelmyer grumbled something about things not in his control and hung up the microphone.

"Did Devon just speak?" asked Cali as she sat down in the front seat with Veronica.

"We never know when it's going to happen," Veronica answered, "but he's intensely interesting without words."

"What do you mean?

"Can't you tell by looking at them?"

Cali looked back. She could see two coonskin hats above the seat. She guessed Warren's was there, too, lower. "They dress funny?"

"They're big cosplayers," Veronica said.

Cali knew about cosplay. Every year at Salt Lake ComicCon thousands of people dressed up as characters from movies and comic books. She had seen the pictures.

"They dress up almost every day. Sometimes it's elaborate, like when they came as The Munsters. They get in trouble with the principal when they do that, so usually they keep it light, like today."

Veronica stood up and called. "Daniel Boone?"

"Davey Crockett," Warren called back.

"Gee Whiz, Daniel Boone was fifty-three years older than Davey Crockett. You'd think you could tell the difference," Marissa yelled.

Veronica looked at Cali and shrugged.

"I love it when they come as three different Doctor Whos," Felicia said. "They do that a lot. Warren looks cute in a Fez."

The excitement from the encounter with the wolves wore off. The chatter on the bus slowed until there was a moment of complete silence. Only the sound of the engine vibrated through the air. Outside, the sun hid just below the mountains in the east lighting the sky a pale blue. Cali sighed in relief at being out of the horrible fog.

"You were so brave," Veronica said, softly.

Veronica meant well, but her words were irritating. "I wasn't brave," Cali said, staring down at her hands.

"But you went with Shelley. No one else would have done that."

"I didn't have a choice," Cali said. "Shelley dragged me out there."

"She did?"

Cali showed her wrist. There was a a bruise forming. "She's strong," she said.

Mr. Fennelmyer was looking up in his mirror and saw. "I'm sorry," he said. "I had no idea she would do that. I knew she'd be all right out there, but you, the new girl? That was wrong of her."

As much as she agreed with Mr. Fennelmyer she didn't like the tone he took. Looking up the aisle Cali saw Shelley lying on her seat exhausted. She was sleeping.

"I think she did need somebody to help her," Cali said, turning back to Mr. Fennelmyer. "I don't know if she could have carried Warren and stayed ahead of the wolves."

Cali closed her eyes. She revisited the scene of the chase in her head. "You should have seen her, Mr. Fennelmyer. She was awesome."

"I think *you're* awesome," Veronica said.

Cali opened her eyes. Veronica's words bothered her. How could a girl who leaps out of an airplane everyday be impressed by anything, let alone a coward like Cali? It was probably just silly talk because Cali was the new girl.

"I'm not awesome. You don't even know me," she said, more harshly than she meant to.

Cali winced at the hurt she saw in Veronica's eyes.

Mr. Fennelmyer heard it, too. There was a moment of awkward silence.

"Tell me," he said, "what is Veronica supposed to think when she sees the new girl carrying a defenseless little boy out of the fog to safety just steps ahead of a ferocious wolf?"

Cali opened her mouth to tell Mr. Fennelmyer that what Veronica didn't see was the fear. The words never came. She closed her mouth. Mr. Fennelmyer *had* accurately described what Veronica saw. What was truer—what she felt, or what Veronica saw?

. . . heroes are made by those who tell the stories . . .

Okay, Dad, she thought. *I think I get it.*

CHAPTER 11 – I WILL SCREAM

Cali contemplated her bravery.

I'm brave if I tell the 'rescue' part of the story and not the 'scared' part. It never occurred to her when she got out of bed that morning that someone would think she was brave. Just going to a new school was about all the bravery she could conjure up.

Cali glanced at Veronica who sat swinging her short legs. She only saw the brave part of the story. Her freckles looked happy on her face. Her bright red hair looked happy on her head. The memory of seeing Veronica drop through the roof hatch onto Freddy made Cali feel happy. She couldn't help smiling.

"What?" Veronica said.

"You call me brave, but I would never catch the bus the way you do."

Veronica smiled, shyly. "Well, you get used to it."

Cali thought about this. "Get used to it?" she said. "I don't think so. I'll never even get used to just riding this bus. Everything about it is so . . ." she paused to search for the word.

"Peculiar?" Mr. Fennelmyer suggested.

"Yes, *peculiar*," Cali said, letting the word roll off her tongue. She had been thinking of 'weird' or 'strange,' but 'peculiar' was exactly the right word.

Finding the right word, said her dad, *is like scratching an itch.*

"Everyone on this bus is peculiar in some way," Cali said. "Are they peculiar because they are on Bus 13, or is Bus 13 peculiar because they are on it?"

"Don't look at me," Veronica said with a shrug. "I'm only in fourth grade."

Cali looked at Mr. Fennelmyer. He was focused on the road. "Mr. Fennelmyer?" she prodded.

"Dang," he said. "You've got too much lawyer in your blood. I was hoping if I ignored the question it would go away."

After a few more moments of silence, Cali said, "Well?"

"I'm thinking," he said a little gruffly. "It's a little bit of both, I think," he finally said. "There is definitely something peculiar about Bus 13. It's like it's bigger on the inside, if you know what I mean." He looked at Cali in the mirror and raised an eyebrow.

It was the second reference to *Dr. Who* that morning. Cali's mom was a *Dr. Who* fan. She always watched old episodes of the show late at night after Cali's bedtime. Cali still caught a few episodes here and there. She knew what the Tardis was.

"Yes, I think you're right," she said.

"But it's definitely the kids, too," he said. "Sometimes kids get on this bus, but then they quit riding."

"So?" Cali asked

"If Bus 13 made kids peculiar they wouldn't quit riding. Only the truly peculiar kids stay."

"But I thought this bus only stopped for kids who are already peculiar."

"That's true," Mr. Fennelmyer said. "But from what I've seen being peculiar is more choice than fate. This bus forces kids to make a decision—keep what makes them special or hide it to be like everyone else."

"He's talking about being normal," Veronica said, rolling her eyes.

"I think normal is the wrong word," said Mr. Fennelmyer, glancing at Veronica. "To me, you're normal. It's just that you don't work very hard at fitting in with the majority. I think that's why you stick with Bus 13."

"No, the kids on this bus *are* weird," Veronica said. "I only keep riding because the other bus drivers won't let me sky dive."

Mr. Fennelmyer and Cali gave Veronica a quizzical look. She grinned.

"People quit riding Bus 13?" Cali asked, turning back to Mr. Fennelmyer.

Mr. Fennelmyer nodded.

"Do any ever come back?"

"No one's ever come back."

"Is that because you won't let them?" Cali couldn't envision someone like Veronica leaving and not coming back unless they just weren't allowed back.

"I don't choose who rides this bus, Cali. Each one of you decides for yourself." Mr. Fennelmyer had a way of quickly glancing up into his mirror where he could see Cali without turning around.

"Once they leave, it's like they don't remember." interrupted Veronica. Her voice was sad. "I'm pretty sure David doesn't even remember my name now."

"He used to ride the bus?"

Veronica smiled and nodded. "He told the best stories. Everyone on the bus would sit close to him to listen. He could make us laugh so loud." Veronica paused. She spoke softer when she talked again. "He was nice to me, too, even though he was in fifth grade and I was in third.

"Once, when I tried to land through the hatch I missed. Mr. Fennelmyer hit the brakes and I rolled off the front of the bus."

"I am so sorry about that," Mr. Fennelmyer said, blushing.

"David got out of the bus to see if I was okay. He helped me gather my chute and my books. He was so nice."

Veronica glanced at Cali. Her cheeks were red. She looked out the window and went on. "A couple of the popular wrestlers at school made friends with him. He quit riding Bus 13 after that. I see him every day at school. He never even looks at me."

Veronica was lost in thought for a few moments. "Why are you so curious about people who quit riding the bus, anyway?"

Cali couldn't find the words to answer that question. Rather than face the feisty Veronica she changed the subject. "Mr. Fennelmyer? You know that wolf, Sheila? Well, she talked to me."

"You named the wolf?" he asked, surprised.

"No, I didn't name her. That's her name. She told me."

"She's a talking wolf?" Mr. Fennelmyer seemed to think this was just too much to believe.

"Why would a talking wolf be any stranger than complete chemistry labs and pipe organs in lunch boxes? Or identical twins who aren't even related to each other?" She looked at Veronica, who sat smiling at her, "Or cute little girls who jump out of airplanes to catch the school bus? Or just the fact that those wolves exist at all, huh? Why is a talking wolf any stranger than any of that?"

Cali's raised voice drew attention. Eyes appeared over the tops of seats. Cali blushed, then ignored them.

"Now, calm down," Mr. Fennelmyer said. "I suppose it's not any stranger, but I just hadn't heard that this wolf talks."

Cali looked back at the still sleeping Shelley. Hadn't she told them anything about her experience with the wolves?

"Well, it's not like the wolf moved her mouth or anything," Cali explained, "but she still told me things, like directly into my mind."

"Well, then," Mr Fennelmyer said. It was as if the wolf talking to Cali without moving its mouth made it normal. "What did she say?"

"She wants to go home."

Please!

Mr. Fennelmyer waited for Cali to go on. She didn't, so he asked, "Where does a wolf live?"

"She's not a wolf. She's a girl. She needs someone to take her place so she can go home." Cali's face was flushed. She knew this didn't make sense. Still, Mr. Fennelmyer would be able to figure it out. He was the driver of Bus 13. The blank look on his face told her that he didn't know what she was talking about.

"Great!" she said angrily. "That's just great. Why is there even an adult on this bus when he can't explain to a kid like me what's going on?"

Mr. Fennelmyer concentrated on the road. Veronica studied her hands in her lap.

"I never should have gotten on this bus," Cali said, plaintively.

Veronica gasped. Her head jerked up. She tried to take Cali's hand. Cali yanked it away. The eyes of everyone on the bus focused on her. She slunk down in her seat.

Finally Mr. Fennelmyer looked at her in the mirror. "You tell me. Why did you get on? I have to admit, I was surprised when you climbed that first step."

Cali was surprised and a little disappointed. She expected Mr. Fennelmyer to automatically list reasons for riding.

He waited for an answer. When Cali couldn't find words he went on.

"I know why all these kids got on, and I even know why the kids who quit riding got on. But, you? You puzzle me."

"Well, I apologize for causing the confusion," Cali sulked. "I'm sure I don't know why I got on either."

That was a lie. She knew. The bus had called to her when the door opened. It offered her every good, beautiful, exciting thing in the world if she would only ride. Well, she had chosen to ride, but Bus 13 had lied to her. All Bus 13 had given her was confusion and fear. Riding Bus 13 was no more than a nightmare.

Veronica looked at Cali. Her eyes brimmed with tears. Cali's words had hurt her. Across the aisle Felicia met her eyes and tried to squash the awkwardness with a smile. Behind Felicia Shelley lay sleeping, oblivious to the drama. A few seats back Jimmy peeked out. He had put his pipes away and was playing his harmonica—a pretty little melody that Cali didn't recognize.

From where she sat only Bric's and Freddy's eyes and the top of Brac's head were visible over the seat tops. They appeared to be arguing about something, but they kept looking in her direction.

Near the back Marty and Marcus were growing a big, green bubble. It floated to the roof where it popped. Tendrils of bubble fell into their hair like silly string. They looked up at her expectantly, hoping they'd impressed her. She almost smiled, but at the last moment gave an 'I am not amused' look, instead. In the very back seat she saw two coonskin hats twitching this way and that as Devon and Marissa carried on a conversation.

Okay, she thought, *maybe 'nightmare' is too harsh a word for Bus 13, but it is definitely*—she thought a moment—*peculiar.*

Cali realized that 'peculiar' was the problem—or, more accurately, the fact that she wasn't peculiar. Every one of these kids had something that made them stand out—something that made them special in a peculiar way. She had nothing. When it came to personality, she was vanilla in an ice cream shop that offered forty spectacular flavors.

"You said you wouldn't have stopped for me this morning, that the bus stopped all by itself. Maybe the bus made a mistake."

"Bus 13 doesn't make mistakes," Mr. Fennelmyer said.

"But there isn't a peculiar bone in my body"

"You don't like us?" Veronica sighed.

"No!" Cali thought a moment. "Yes! Oh, I don't know. I'm so confused."

Just then a paper airplane, the kind with the blunt nose, zipped by her head. Banking sharply it narrowly missed the windshield and came back. It circled twice over her head before nosediving into her lap. She saw a sentence written in red ink disappearing into the center fold. She unfolded the airplane and read:

> *You can check out any time you want, but you can never leave.*
> *--The Eagles, Hotel California*

"Oh, I love that song," said Veronica.

Cali liked it, too. Her dad still had the vinyl album although now they listened to it on the mp3 player. Her Dad was offended when she called it a golden oldie.

It's definitely golden, he said, *but not so old.*

Cali turned in her seat to look to the back of the bus. Bric, Brac, and Freddy stared back at her. The message had to have come from them. Only they would be thorough enough to give the reference. Bric raised an eyebrow and nodded to give emphasis.

Cali turned and dropped back into her seat. "You see?" She addressed the ceiling, Mr. Fennelmyer, nobody in particular. "It's this kind of thing I don't understand. Are they just teasing me or are they serious? And how did they get the paper airplane to land in my lap?"

Veronica and Mr. Fennelmyer gave her worried looks. Mr. Fennelmyer glanced over his shoulder, clearly curious about what was written on the paper airplane. he couldn't read it and drive at the same time.

"If one more crazy thing happens, I'll scream."

Veronica caught Mr. Fennelmyer's eye in the mirror. She looked alarmed. "Who do we pick up next?" she asked.

"Rosalie" answered Mr. Fennelmyer.

Their eyes widened.

"Oh, dear," they said in unison.

CHAPTER 12 – OH, DEAR

Cali looked at Veronica and then at Mr. Fennelmyer. "'Oh, dear,' what?"

Veronica shrugged. "Nothing." She turned and looked out the window.

Giving up on Veronica, Cali eyed Mr. Fennelmyer. He looked uncomfortable.

"What she said," he said.

Cali took a big breath, trying hard not to scream. "I think," she said, pausing to breathe, "somebody ought to tell me about Rosalie *before* she floats out of the sky, rides up on a wolf, or pulls a giant squid out of her lunchbox."

She was going to get no answer from Mr. Fennelmyer or Veronica, so Cali turned to Felicia. Felicia sat quietly looking out the window careful not to appear to be eavesdropping. She made the mistake of glancing at Cali.

"Oh, it's nothing like that," she said, breaking into a smile. "She's actually the cutest little fourth grader you've ever seen."

"Then why, 'Oh, dear?'" Cali asked, before Felicia could look away.

"Well, she *is* a character," Felicia said.

"She's peculiar, right?" Cali asked, narrowing her eyes.

"Just a little." Felicia shrugged. "It's nothing to worry about."

"She worries me," Jimmy said, poking out his head.

"She downright scares the heck out of me," said Brac, standing up.

"That's because you're her boyfriend," called Marissa from the back.

"I'm *not* her boyfriend," Brac yelled.

"She *thinks* you are," Marissa responded.

Felicia stood and half turned. "You guys aren't helping!" She was dangerously close to being a little upset. Having silenced the rest of the bus, she sat back down. "I really think that they joke around too much. They don't understand how confusing all this is to you."

"Oh, I underst—" started Jimmy.

"Shut it," yelled Felicia, sweetly. Looking at Cali she said, "Rosalie is hard to describe. You'll just have to see for yourself."

The bus slowed and stopped. Cali didn't dare to look out the window. She held her breath as the door opened, wincing at the sound of each footstep on the stairs.

"G'morning, Rosalie," said Mr. Fennelmyer.

"Good morn—," Rosalie began. She saw Cali and froze.

"Rosalie, meet Cali," said Mr. Fennelmyer. "Cali. Rosalie."

Cali looked into the brownest eyes she had ever seen. Although she was sitting their eyes were level. Rosalie's black hair curled around her neck. She wasn't any taller than Veronica. She acted like a sixth grader.

Rosalie scrutinized Cali. Turning to Mr. Fennelmyer she said, "You didn't tell me we were getting a new girl."

"I didn't know, now, did I? You know I never know when—"

Rosalie cut him off. "She looks scared. What have you been telling her about me?"

"You know it's my policy not to talk about Bus 13 children—"

"What has he been telling you about me?" she asked, not letting Mr. Fennelmyer finish. "Whatever it was is probably not true, or at least it's exaggerated."

Taking Cali's hand she tugged her out of her seat. "Come sit by me so I can tell you the way it really is. I'm not the six-headed monster these bozos think I am."

Rosalie wasn't as frightening as Cali thought she would be. She looked at Felicia for support. Felicia winked and motioned with her head as if to say, 'Go ahead. We bozos will be here if you need us.'

Rosalie tugged her up the aisle. Cali glanced back and saw Veronica peeking over the seat-top between her two hands. Her eyes were wide. Jimmy scooted away from the aisle against the wall of the bus. He glanced at them timidly as they passed.

What about this little girl frightens them so much?

Rosalie pushed her into a seat and blocked the way out with her little body. She turned to look at Brac, two seats back.

"Hello, Brac," she said, sweetly.

"Ahhh," yelled Brac. "Leave me alone."

The flirting smile on Rosalie's face turned into an angry pout. Something in Rosalie's expression sent a shiver down Cali's spine— not the expression itself, something behind it, some power she could feel.

"You know, I could *make* you like me," Rosalie said, low and menacingly. Something in the air came alive. There was a buzz, or was it a humming? Cali couldn't tell; whatever it was wasn't natural. Cali got ready to scream.

"Rosalie."

It was the voice Cali had heard that morning as she was trying to decide whether to get on the bus—the big and gentle voice with sparkles. This time it was stern. Rosalie flinched as if she had touched an electric fence. Mr. Fennelmyer had turned around. His glasses glinted with unnatural light.

Rosalie's expression morphed instantly into remorse. Cali saw shock in her eyes, and then sadness. Just for a moment it looked like Rosalie was going to cry.

"Brac," she said solemnly, blinking away tears. "I would never *make* you like me." Her face brightened again. With a glint in her brown eyes she added, "But one day you just will."

Rosalie slipped into the seat beside Cali. "Boys," she said. "Always making us girls make fools out of ourselves."

She smiled at Cali and studied her face. Rosalie's smile faded. "You're terrified of me, aren't you?" she asked, sadly. The sadness took on an angry tone. "What did they tell you about me?"

Instinctively, Cali scooted away from Rosalie. It was true, she was terrified.

Rosalie noticed, and her eyes narrowed in anger. Cali cringed. Rosalie's anger hit an emergency relief valve. Her eyes became sad again. Tears welled up, and this time a few splashed onto her cheeks.

Rosalie's moods had changed so quickly and so many times since she had boarded the bus. Cali expected the tears to dry into another emotion momentarily. The tears stayed. Rosalie wiped them onto the back of her hand and then onto her jeans. Pity found its way through Cali's fear. Whatever else she was was, Rosalie was still a little girl.

Fighting back her tears Rosalie sniffed, "Mr. Fennelmyer promised me he wouldn't tell about me; that he would give me a chance with the next new person. He promised."

Beneath the drama, Cali felt genuine hurt.

Cali took a deep breath. "He didn't break his promise," she said. "He didn't say anything about you."

"Really?"

"Yes, really."

Rosalie brightened up a little. "Then why are you so afraid of me?" Her eyes narrowed again. "Someone else talked, didn't they."

"We didn't tell her nothing," yelled Warren from the back of the bus. "And we're not afraid of you!"

"Why *would* we be afraid of you?" said Felicia from up front.

"The people on this bus have really good ears," Cali mumbled.

"Oh, it's just the way Bus 13 is," Rosalie said. Her anger was gone if someone flipped a switch. "Keeps us all honest." A sly smile came to her lips. "But I can fix that." Leaning in she whispered, "I've been practicing."

Rosalie sat back and stared at the seatback in front of her. Her eyes went blank. There was a distinct buzz in the air. Cali looked for a fly. Rosalie's eyes rolled back and her chin dropped to her chest. Before Cali could call for help Rosalie's eyes flicked open.

"I love you, Brac!" she yelled. There was a touch of ecstasy in her voice.

This sudden declaration confused Cali. Brac didn't respond. The bus was so silent that Cali sat up to see where everyone had gone. They were there. Bric, Brac, and Freddy looked her way, warily. Marissa and Warren were hanging over the seat in front of them watching with interest.

"What's going on?" Cali asked.

"It's a soundproof bubble," Rosalie said. "Mr. Fennelmyer will be mad at me, but this is something that I know doesn't hurt anybody." She thought for a moment, and then added, "And it doesn't make me very sleepy."

"A soundproof bubble?"

Rosalie nodded.

"You made it?"

Rosalie nodded again. "Try it. Yell something rude at Mr. Fennelmyer."

"No."

"You don't believe me?"

It wasn't that. Cali just didn't believe in being rude.

Rosalie didn't have a problem with that. "Mr. Fennelmyer drives like a blind monkey," she yelled.

When Cali sat up to see Mr. Fennelmyer's reaction Rosalie took her arm, "Don't look up there. You'll catch his eye and he'll know something's up. Just yell something."

From her glimpse over the seat Cali had seen no reaction from Mr. Fennelmyer. Not able to resist the temptation she called out, "Mr. Fennelmyer? I'm going to be sick." That wasn't very rude, but she knew Mr. Fennelmyer would respond if he could hear. There was no response.

Rosalie looked at Cali, grinning. Cali smiled. She couldn't help it— this was cool.

"It won't last very long, though," Rosalie said. A mischievous look came to her eyes. She yelled, "Bric, Brac, and Freddy are the Three Morons."

"What?" Bric yelled. "Who's a moron?" Apparently he only caught the last word.

"Oh, poop," giggled Rosalie, sliding down into her seat.

"They can hear us now?" asked Cali.

"Hear what?" asked Freddy.

"I told you it wouldn't last long," whispered Rosalie.

"What have you been up to?" asked Brac. "Have you been doing magic?"

"That's highly unlikely," said Bric. "She's not sleeping, is she?"

"I don't think we can trust that response," said Brac. "How do we know she sleeps in every single case of magic? We haven't proven that scientifically, now have we?"

"But our observations lead us to believe—"

"Belief is not always truth."

Rosalie rolled her eyes as the argument heated up. "Boys are so boring. Want to see something else?" There was that charming, mischievous grin again, slightly lopsided toward the dimple on her left cheek.

Cali nodded.

Rosalie lifted her right hand in front of her with fingers spread as if she were holding a grapefruit. Her eyes narrowed in concentration. Cali heard a buzzing—or was it more of a humming?—in the air. The hairs on the back of her arms stood up like during a summer lightning storm. A moment later candle flames poofed to life at the tips of Rosalie's fingers.

Cali stared at the flames in disbelief. They hovered a fraction of an inch above each finger and danced lightly with the air movement

"Oh, poop," said Rosalie in a strange little voice. It took effort, but Cali tore her eyes from the flames. She looked at Rosalie just in time to see her eyes roll back, then close. She went limp and her hand dropped. Leaning slowly Rosalie toppled into Cali's lap. The flames at Rosalie's fingertips kept burning just long enough that the fabric of Rosalie's shirt started to melt and smoke.

"Help! Help, fire!" yelled Cali. She beat out the flames with her hand.

She felt the bus making an emergency stop. Bric and Freddy shot by her seat as their unrestrained bodies followed the second law of motion. They had moved into the aisle to come to Cali's aid before Mr. Fennelmyer hit the brakes. Cali heard a thump and a grunt.

"Get off of me," Bric said.

"About time somebody else was the floor," answered Freddy.

Veronica and Felicia appeared over the seat in front of Cali. Marty and Marcus stared down from behind her seat. Bric, Marissa, and Warren vied for position beside her.

"Uh oh, magic," said Bric, rather casually. "She's going to be in trouble."

"There was fire," Cali said in a small voice.

"Oh, did she do that fire from her fingers thing?" Warren pushed his head between Bric and Marissa. "I've been wanting to see that for a long time." He looked disappointed he had missed it.

"Then, she passed out," finished Cali. She looked into the faces around her. None of them appeared worried, except for Felicia. She was looking at Cali, not Rosalie.

"Move aside," yelled Mr. Fennelmyer. He pulled some kids out of the way and squeezed between others. He finally appeared at Cali's side with a fire extinguisher.

"Too late. The fire's out," said Marissa.

"Rosalie was doing her finger fire trick again," said Bric.

"I wish she'd teach us that," Marty said, looking at Marcus.

"Yep, that'd mean no more Bunsen burners for us," Marcus replied.

"She promised me she wouldn't do magic for the entire month," Mr. Fennelmyer said, disappointed. "It's only been two weeks."

"She only promised she would *try*," said Brac. "I remember. It seemed odd to me that you would accept such a promise. She's going to win every time with a promise like that. You can't prove she didn't *try* not to use magic."

"Well, why didn't you bring that up at the time?" growled Mr. Fennelmyer.

"I think it's important to let people learn from experience," said Brac.

Mr. Fennelmyer opened his mouth to reply. Cali interrupted.

"What is wrong with you people? Rosalie was on fire, and now she's unconscious. Doesn't anyone care?"

Everyone went quiet and looked at Cali like they just remembered she was there.

Felicia spoke first. "Rosalie's just fine. She always falls asleep after she performs—" She hesitated, not wanting to say the word in front of Cali.

"Magic?" Cali said, saying the word for her. "I distinctly heard somebody say magic. You're telling me that Rosalie can do magic?"

The kids looked at each other. Finally, Mr. Fennelmyer cleared his throat. Marcus stopped him by raising his hand.

"If you please, Mr. Fennelmyer, magic is best dealt with by children."

Mr. Fennelmyer closed his mouth and nodded.

"There isn't much to explain, really," said Marcus. "Rosalie can make things happen by thinking about them. 'Magic' is the only word that comes close to describing the phenomenon."

"It's like a gift she has," said Marissa, her blue eyes showing a hint of jealousy.

"More like a curse," said Felicia.

"Definitely a curse," agreed Mr. Fennelmyer.

Cali struggled to keep up with them. Magic? Gifts? Curses? None of this explained a girl lying unconscious in her lap—or the wet spot on her jeans near Rosalie's mouth. Rosalie was drooling.

"What is wrong with Rosalie right now?" Cali asked impatiently.

"She falls asleep whenever she uses magic," chimed in Warren. "It's a bummer, except that it's funny when she falls off her seat."

Marty and Brac gave a little laugh.

Felicia gave them a reproving look. "She gets hurt when that happens. I don't think it's very funny."

"So what do we do?" asked Cali.

"Well, that's about as good a spot as she's ever passed out," said Freddy.

"Yep, she looks comfy enough," added Marissa.

"You won't be able to wake her, but," Mr. Fennelmyer hesitated here, "you say it was the finger fire trick?"

Bric nodded.

"Then I suspect she'll wake up pretty quick," finished Mr. Fennelmyer. "She's getting better at that one."

"You're just going to leave her in my lap—" started Cali. Mr. Fennelmyer, checking his watch, interrupted.

"By golly, I think we are actually going to be late today. Philip won't like that. Nope, not at all. Everyone in your seats." Anxiously, he hurried towards the front of the bus.

"Philip?" shouted Brac. "Your boss's name is Philip?"

"You heard nothing," Mr. Fennelmyer yelled back.

Brac looked at Cali. "He won't tell us anything about who he really works for," he said, confidentially.

"But we're going to get it out of him eventually," added Bric.

"You better write that down," said Marty.

"Already done," replied Marcus, shoving a mini-notebook into his shirt pocket.

Everyone returned to their seats and Cali considered crying as she was left alone with Rosalie. Felicia suddenly reappeared looking over the seat in front of her.

"Here," she said, placing a folded paper towel under the corner of Rosalie's mouth where she was drooling. "That should be more comfortable." She gave Cali a sympathetic smile. As she was turning, she stopped and thought a moment. "Um, when Rosalie wakes up, which should be in a minute or two, she might be a little grumpy."

"Ornery," Brac corrected.

Felicia shrugged. "But it won't last long."

CHAPTER 13 – THE MAGIC OF ROSALIE

Cali found herself alone, again. Well, not quite alone—a sleeping, drooling girl was lying in her lap. Not just any girl; a diminutive, unpredictable girl who could do—Cali hesitated at the word—*magic*.

Cali didn't want to believe it, but she had seen it.

Seeing may be believing, but that doesn't mean what you see is true, her mother said.

Cali never understood what her mother meant by that. She thought about it now. She had seen so much on this bus. Was any of it true? Reason told her that it wasn't. It just couldn't be. What, then, could explain what she had seen? She was dreaming was the easiest explanation. She touched the bruise on her arm and flinched. No, not a dream.

Environmental factors could affect the senses. They caused mirages in the desert and UFO sightings in the skies. Marty and Marcus had filled the bus with gases from the chemical laboratory they carried in their lunchbox. Those gases could be having all kinds of effects on her brain.

Cali smiled, relieved by this explanation for a moment. What would explain the existence of a chemistry laboratory that was far too big to fit into a lunchbox? She had seen that before there were any gases. A scream began rising in her throat.

"Felicia?" she called in one last hope.

There was movement in the seat in front of her. Felicia's hands appeared on top of the seat before her face did. "Yes?"

"How much longer until we get to school?"

Felicia thought a moment. "Unless we pick up anyone else unexpectedly, like—" she hesitated.

"Like me?" Cali offered.

"Yes, like you," Felicia smiled apologetically, "there's only one more stop before the school."

"And the school is Red Canyon Elementary in Warburton, right?" She needed to be sure.

"That's the one," Felicia said.

"Is Red Canyon Elementary a *normal* school?" Cali asked.

Felicia maintained her perpetual smile even as an emotion flickered through her eyes.

"I would say that Red Canyon Elementary is normal." After another thoughtful pause she added, "Decidedly normal."

This was exactly what Cali hoped to hear, but the flicker of—Cali decided to go with 'apprehension'—on Felicia's face made her wonder.

As the bus slowed to a stop Rosalie stirred and mumbled something about a puppy.

"She's waking up," Felicia said. Turning to sit down she added, "And here comes our own *luchador*."

Luchador? thought Cali.

She heard a clamor at the front of the bus.

"Forearm slam into headlock," said a voice.

"Ahhhhh," yelled another.

"Don't you two ever stop?" asked Mr. Fennelmyer.

"*Lucha libre* is a life style," said the first boy. "Not just a sport."

"We must prepare for our fame," said the second boy.

"Seems like Arnold always gets the good role," said Mr. Fennelmyer. "All you get, Miguel, is beat up."

"We all must play our roles," said the second voice. "Besides, I can do *this*."

Cali heard an *oof*.

"Massive head butt? It'll give you a headache," said Mr. Fennelmyer.

"He is bigger than me, but his belly is soft," said Miguel.

Cali wanted to stand and see what was going on, but Rosalie was still in her lap. Rosalie's eyes were starting to flicker.

"You'll want to be quiet back there," Mr. Fennelmyer warned. "Rosalie will be waking up soon."

"What?" Arnold said. "She did magic without us?"

"It was to impress the new girl," Veronica chimed in.

"What? A new girl?"

Cali heard clomping up the aisle. Two Hispanic boys appeared next to her seat. Their smiles were big and their eyes bright.

"Arnold the Destroyer," said the bigger boy. He looked to be in fifth grade, but he was bigger than Cali. He bowed with elegance.

"And Miguel the Monster," said the smaller boy. He was far shorter and skinnier than Arnold. Maybe third grade.

"Monster? You mean mouse," Arnold said, grabbing Miguel in a headlock.

"Ahhhh," yelled Miguel, still smiling.

Rosalie sat up, wiping her mouth on the back of her arm. Her hair stuck out on the side she had lain on.

"Uh oh," someone from behind said. Cali wasn't sure if it was Bric, Brac, or Freddy.

"Arnold . . ." Mr. Fennelmyer warned, but he got no further. As Miguel struggled, Arnold swiveled with him and they both knocked against Rosalie. Rosalie whined, and with her whine another sound—the angry humming of bees from a hive Cali had once accidentally disturbed.

Arnold and Miguel didn't hear the warning. Seeing an opportunity to impress the new girl, Miguel hooked his foot behind Arnold's leg and pushed backward. They both fell into Rosalie. They realized where they were and reacted as if Rosalie was a hive of bees.

Arnold pushed Miguel into the seat across the aisle and turned to face Rosalie. He gave a sheepish grin, but his eyes showed he was just a little worried.

He started to utter words of apology, but Rosalie leaped out of her seat. She glared up at him, her chest to his belly. Cali definitely heard a buzzing this time. Something moved the air.

"*Rosalie*," Mr. Fennelmyer said, too late, in his big voice. "Somebody catch her," he yelled and he hit the brakes.

Cali leaned out into the aisle with her arms outstretched as Rosalie's eyes rolled back and she collapsed. The momentum as the bus braked pulled Cali from her seat. Cali landed on top of Rosalie with her arms wrapped around her.

"Oh, wow," said Felicia, regaining her balance. "Nice save!"

Rosalie was out cold. Cali was nose to nose with her. She struggled to get her arms out from under Rosalie. Arnold was yelling, "My arms! My arms!"

"What is it?" asked Brac.

"Yeah, what'd she do?" yelled Warren, excitedly.

"My arms don't work," Arnold cried. "They're broken."

Arnold the Destroyer, in a complete panic, was a pitiful, amusing thing to see.

"She broke them? Do they hurt?" Miguel asked, inspecting Arnold's arms closely.

"No, I can't even feel them," Arnold cried.

At the word 'broken' Devon rushed to Arnold's side.

"Out of the way," Marissa called. "Devon just learned First Aid in scouts last week."

Devon knelt on the seat at Arnold's side. He lifted one of his arms, then dropped it. It fell limply and bounced against Arnold's side. Everyone in the bus winced, except Arnold. He really didn't feel a thing.

"Really?" Mr. Fennelmyer said. "That's what they taught you in boy scouts?" He stood back, unable to get by Rosalie and Cali, or Veronica, Jimmy, and Felicia, who had squeezed in beside them.

"They aren't broken," Devon said. "They just don't work."

"That's what I said," wailed Arnold. "They're broken."

"That's right," said Felicia. "They just don't work. Rosalie would never actually hurt anyone."

"You can't use your arms, cousin?" Miguel asked, a gleam in his eyes.

"No, they don't work," Arnold cried.

"How about now?" Miguel said, and poked Arnold's belly.

"No."

"And now?" Miguel slapped Arnold on the cheek. There was no meanness in the action, just delight. He looked like a boy who had just learned he has superpowers.

"No," cried Arnold.

"How about now?" Miguel knelt on the seat, wrapped an arm around Arnold's head, and gave him a set of serious noogies.

Arnold allowed Miguel to give the noogies until he realized Miguel was taking advantage.

"Ahhh! Stop it. Stop it," he yelled. He tried to stand to get away. Without his arms he had no balance or control. Devon leaned out of the way. Arnold fell across the aisle onto the empty seat before rolling onto the floor.

Miguel stood up on the seat with his arms raised in victory. Everyone except Mr. Fennelmyer and Cali cheered. Shelley was still sleeping and doing a little drooling of her own.

"For heaven's sake," yelled Mr. Fennelmyer. "Miguel, get off the seat. Devon, Freddy, help Arnold off the floor." He took off his hat and ran his fingers across his flat top trying to compose himself. "I can't remember the last time we had such a crazy morning."

"March 22nd, last year?" Jimmy suggested.

"It was the 21st," Bric corrected. Felicia nodded her agreement.

Mr. Fennelmyer stopped in thought with his hand on his head. "Good heavens," he said. "This one may get worse, yet. Do you realize we drive straight to school from here, and," he checked his watch, "we're late? You know we can't be late."

"So, drive fast," suggested Brac.

Mr. Fennelmyer stared at Brac in exasperation. "For such a smart kid you aren't thinking. We have Rosalie passed out on the floor and Arnold with arms that don't work. If we're late, or if we get caught in this chaos, it'll be the end of Bus 13. I'll be out of a job and you'll be riding regular buses."

The bus went silent as what Mr. Fennelmyer said sunk in.

"So, anyone have any ideas?" asked Mr. Fennelmyer, breaking the silence.

"You're asking us?" said Freddy. "You're the adult here."

"I'm just the bus driver. You kids are the ones with the genius IQs."

"Wait, I've never even had an IQ test," said Freddy. "You think I'm a genius?"

"I don't think you're a genius," said Brac. "You don't understand the first thing about the intertidal zone or sponges."

"I, at least, have a sense of humor," Bric chimed in. "I can accept the humor of square sponges in the sea. It's well known that geniuses have great senses of humor."

Mr. Fennelmyer rolled his eyes. "How about you, Jimmy? You got anything?"

"I'm afraid even Bach would be pressed for a solution to this situation," he said, looking troubled.

Mr. Fennelmyer looked at Marty and Marcus next.

"We just make green liquids and gases."

Marissa spoke up before Mr. Fennelmyer got to them. "I knew we should have dressed as Doctor Who today. This is exactly his line of expertise."

"If you're talking about Matt Smith," said Devon.

"What? No, definitely David Tennant."

Marissa and Devon were in a stare-off when Warren spoke up. "I think the best Doctor Who in this situation would be Tom Baker, the fourth doctor."

Everyone on the bus stared at Warren. Warren squirmed a little.

"You know, the one with the curly hair and long scarf."

"We *know*," Bric yelled, "but why on Earth do you think he's the best Doctor Who?"

This ignited a bus-wide argument on the various Doctor Whos. SpongeBob came up in there somewhere, but was immediately squashed.

Mr. Fennelmyer, looking ill, lowered his head and rubbed his temples

Shelley woke up, lifted herself from the seat, and stretched like a dog. She looked around at the arguing occupants of Bus 13, not understanding and not appearing to care. Felicia and Veronica watched the proceedings like they were watching Saturday morning cartoons.

It was all too much for Cali. She focused all of her attention on Rosalie. It was a way of coping with the overwhelming.

Her mother had told her, *In law school when I thought all was lost I learned to focus on one thing I had control over. Maybe it was reading a book, or clipping my toenails—it didn't matter what so long as I had control over it.*

Could Rosalie be made more comfortable? She got Rosalie flat on her back, straightened her shirt, and then placed her hands across her chest. Cali felt like a little girl playing with a doll. It was comforting.

When she looked up, Mr. Fennelmyer was watching her.

"What do you think?" he said.

Problems are always easier to solve if you break them down into their most simple form," her father said.

"It seems to me that Rosalie is the only one who can fix Arnold's arms. We have to wait for her to wake up."

Mr. Fennelmyer's eyes lit up. "That's the first sensible thing I've heard." He yelled, "Listen up!"

No one paid attention. He put two fingers in his mouth and whistled a piercing note. The bus fell silent with everyone's eyes on him.

"Only Rosalie can fix Arnold's arms, but she might be asleep for an hour after pulling a stunt like that. We have to wake her up somehow."

"You want me to play something really loud?" asked Jimmy.

"No. You'd only kill us all with the volume." He looked at Marty and Marcus. "I do believe it's up to you."

"Us?" asked Marcus.

"It would have to be a wake up potion," said Marty, sounding intrigued.

"Do scientists do potions?" Marcus asked.

"No. *Wizards* do," said Marty, reverently.

Marty and Marcus looked at each other. Their moment had come. Turning, they marched to their seat where their chemistry set awaited.

CHAPTER 14 – ARRIVAL

Arnold was still flummoxed at how to get up without his arms. Devon and Freddy managed to pull him out from between the two seats.

"Come on. Stand up. It's your arms that don't work; your legs are fine," Freddy said.

Arnold looked as miserable as Miguel looked enthusiastic.

"We can change our act," Miguel said. "You can spin so that your arms swing out like blades. We will be *Miguel and the Human Chopper.*"

Arnold frowned and looked away.

"I'm going to drive while you guys create the potion," Mr. Fennelmyer said over the intercom. "Maybe somebody up there," he glanced up, skeptically, "will have had enough amusement for today and let us get the potion made *and* arrive on time."

Cali stayed at Rosalie's side even though it was uncomfortable in the narrow aisle. She could see how dirty the floor was from her vantage point—crushed corn chips and crinkled candy wrappers lurked under the seats.

"It's very kind of you to be so concerned for Rosalie," Felicia said from behind Cali.

Cali felt a twinge of guilt. Taking care of Rosalie was simply something sane to do amid all the craziness around her. Besides, the thought of leaving Rosalie lying in the aisle was distasteful.

Cali looked into Rosalie's sleeping face as it rocked back and forth with the motion of the bus. To be able to do magic, but to fall on your face unconscious each time you did was—well—a curse.

"This isn't the first time Rosalie's passed out into the aisle," Felicia said, trying to make Cali feel better.

"Or the second, or the third," Veronica added.

"Why does she try to—" Cali didn't like to say the word *magic* out loud, "do stuff when she knows she will pass out?"

There was silence as Felicia thought.

Cali put her hand over Rosalie's heart. After a moment she felt it beating faintly.

"This is very private, but for some reason I feel like I can trust you." Felicia lowered her voice to a whisper.

Cali wasn't sure if on Bus 13 a whisper would make a difference.

"Rosalie has a difficult home life. There are some," Felicia hesitated, "addiction problems."

By 'addiction problems' Cali understood Felicia to mean one or both of Rosalie's parents had problems. What did that have to do with Rosalie using her 'gift' when she knew she would pass out?

Cali's heard Veronica speaking to Mr. Fennelmyer. "If our—er— wizards actually manage to wake up Rosalie in time—"

"Oh, they will," Mr. Fennelmyer cut in, anxiously. "They have to."

"—she will have to use *magic* to fix his arms," Veronica stared knowingly at Mr. Fennelmyer.

"Yes." He glanced at Veronica. The expression on her face made him uncomfortable. "What? What's wrong?"

"She'll have to use *magic* to fix his arms," Veronica repeated.

Mr. Fennelmyer suddenly got it. "Oh, good heavens," he said. "She'll pass out again." He grabbed the microphone. "Marty? Marcus? Make sure you make enough for two doses."

A loud rumbling sound shook the back of the bus. Mr. Fennelmyer looked up to see green gas billowing its way upward.

Grabbing the microphone he yelled, "Windows! Windows!"

He needn't have bothered. The kids knew the drill. Windows clacked down and heads appeared outside amid coughing and gagging.

"Sulphur nitrate? Really, Marcus?"

"Hey, it's the pressure. I'm not used to making things under pressure."

"But how could you possibly confuse sulphur nitrate for ammonium carbonate? That's a noob mistake."

"Well, I don't know if it's any worse than accidentally filling the bus with nitrous oxide last month," said Marcus. "You about got all of us sent to Principal Kay because we couldn't stop giggling when we got to school."

"It wasn't that bad," said Marty.

"Not that bad? Mr. Fennelmyer was still laughing when he picked us up in the afternoon."

"Residual gas in the bus, I suppose," mumbled Marty.

"That was the funnest bus ride ever," said Warren, from across the aisle. "I wish you'd do it again."

"Rosalie, you are so lucky you are sleeping through this," Cali whispered. Her eyes burned and there was a horrible, bitter taste in the back of her mouth.

"We're only ten minutes out," Mr. Fennelmyer called over the intercom. "Try again—and for heaven's sake, get it right this time." He had his own window open and the driver's fans on high.

"Hey, there are only human beings on this bus," Marty said, standing up. "No superheroes." Everyone flinched at the sound of rattling bottles and tubes.

Shelley swiveled in her seat. Kneeling, she looked back. "Speak for yourself, mere human." Her voice was part growl. She gave Cali a grin and a slow wink as she sat down.

Cali stared at Shelley in surprise. Pressure situations seemed to wake her up a little.

"You stand corrected, Marty," Bric said, laughing.

"Uh oh, traffic," Jimmy said, looking out the window.

Bus 13 had reached the houses that spilled outside the Warburton City limits. There was a car ahead of them and another pulling out of a driveway.

"Is all the gas gone?" Veronica asked. "Green gas spilling out the windows is hard to explain. Caitlyn's mom called the police *and* poison control last time, remember?"

"How could I forget?" said Mr. Fennelmyer. "When I saw the police lights flashing behind us I thought it was over."

"How'd you get out of that one?" asked Jimmy.

"It was easier than I thought. 'Green gas? What could she possible mean?'" Mr. Fennelmyer said, recreating what he had said to the policeman. Glancing in his mirror at Cali he added, "I mean who's going to believe a report like that?"

"So, you lied?" asked Veronica.

"No, I just asked a simple question. The officer made his own assumptions about the quality of Caitlyn's mom's eyesight."

"That's still pretty tricky," said Veronica.

"But impressive," called Freddy.

"I was in a tight spot." More quietly, Mr. Fennelmyer added, "And I think you kids have had a negative influence on me."

Mr. Fennelmyer brought the bus to a stop at the railroad tracks. He turned on his hazard lights, and opened the door. Absentmindedly he reached for his window, but it was already open. "Holy Moly," he said. "Look."

"What? A train?" asked Veronica. Everyone but Cali and Rosalie looked out the windows.

"There's never any trains here," said Bric. "I always wonder why you stop and go through the whole procedure."

"Because I'm a good bus driver," Mr. Fennelmyer said, "but that's not the point. Look up there." He pointed at the busy street that intersected their road another block up.

"I don't see anything," said Felicia.

"That *is* the point. Bus 6 always—*always*—drives by when we reach the tracks. It's not there. That means it's already gone by. That means we're late." Looking in the mirror he yelled, "Please tell me you've got it, Marcus."

Another rumble came from the back of the bus. Mr. Fennelmyer's eyes showed complete and utter panic.

As windows clacked down Marty yelled, "Calm down. It's okay. Not all rumbles are bad. That was a good rumble. Won't you guys ever learn the difference?"

"You . . . you mean you got it?" Mr. Fennelmyer said, hopefully.

"Yep," Marcus said proudly. "That was the rumble of success."

"I don't really think there's a difference," Shelley whispered to Cali and Felicia.

"Two doses?" asked Mr. Fennelmyer.

Marcus held up two small vials.

"Well, hurry up, then. We're only three minutes out."

Marcus hurried up the aisle with the vials. Cali moved to a seat to get out of his way.

"You're sure what you made is completely safe?" Mr. Fennelmyer asked worriedly.

"You said make something to wake her, not something safe," Marcus said.

"Wha—?" Mr. Fennelmyer began.

"Kidding," Marcus said with a grin. "We make things that stink and things that are noisy, but we don't make dangerous things."

"Mom would kill us if we did," added Marty.

"This is a potion called *Wakeupus Nowimus*," Marcus said with pride. He saw Mr. Fennelmyer staring at him suspiciously in the mirror. "It's basically smelling salts on steroids," he added, "but it sounds better in Latin."

"That's not Latin," Jimmy said. He mouthed *Wakeupus Nowimus* and then translated, "Wake up now?"

"You know Latin?" Felicia asked, impressed.

"No," Jimmy said, "it's not Latin. He just made that up."

"That's what wizards do," said Marcus, "make things up."

"Then just do it," Mr. Fennelmyer said. "We're almost there." Up ahead Red Canyon Elementary sat in all its one-story glory on its city block.

Marcus straddled Rosalie and bent over to hold the vial near her nose. "*Wakeupus nowimus*," he called in his best Gandalf voice, and pulled out the stopper.

It worked, maybe too well. Rosalie's eyes flew open. She would have recoiled from the vial, but the floor was in the way. Instead, she sat up with a swiftness that impressed even Shelley and gave Marcus a mighty shove. She wasn't sure what he had done to her, but she didn't like it. Marcus's feet left the ground as he flew backward. Both vials flew through the air. Marcus landed on Marissa, who was coming up the aisle to watch. They both went to the floor. There was the tinkling sound of a small glass object breaking.

Looking down at Marissa Freddy grinned. "Another human floor. We'll have to start a club."

"The vials," Mr. Fennelmyer called. "I heard something break." He looked like he was having a heart attack.

"One broken vial at my feet," Jimmy said, looking down.

"Oh, no," Mr. Fennelmyer said, weakly.

"I caught one," Devon said,. from behind Marcus and Marissa. They were untangling themselves and getting to their feet. "It bounced off my coonskin cap and landed in my hand."

"Which one is it?" Mr. Fennelmyer asked.

"It's still got the stopper in it," said Devon.

"Thank heavens," said Mr. Fennelmyer and he slumped down in his seat in relief.

Felicia stepped in. "Rosalie, would you please fix Arnold's arms? You might need to hurry a little."

"Fix Arnold's arms?" Rosalie looked ornery *and* confused.

Arnold stood up more desperate than angry. He swung his useless arms to show her.

Rosalie gasped. "Oh, no!" Without another word she focused on Arnold, squinting her eyes. The air buzzed. The hair on everyone's arms stood on end. Arnold raised his arms, a look of euphoria on his face.

"Oh poo—," Rosalie said as her eyes rolled back.

"Catch her, somebody," called Mr. Fennelmyer.

Rosalie fell right into Arnold's repaired arms.

"I bet you're glad you fixed my arms," Arnold said to the unconscious Rosalie as he laid her down in the aisle.

"I wonder if she sleeps this well at night," said Miguel.

"Don't lay her on her face," Cali said. Felicia was preparing to say the same thing. Cali pushed Arnold back and rolled Rosalie over. It wasn't easy in that narrow aisle. Cali fell backwards against Jimmy as the bus turned the corner.

"Sorry," Cali said, embarrassed.

"Any time," Jimmy said, grunting as he pushed against her back to get her on her feet.

"Hooray," Mr. Fennelmyer said. "We made it."

Three other buses were lined up in the bus lane at the side of the school. Their red lights flashed as kids streamed out of them. Mr. Fennelmyer turned into the bus lane, eased to a stop behind the third bus, and. glanced up into the mirror. He looked like a man who had just arrived on dry land after escaping a sinking boat. The expression lasted about one second. He noticed that Rosalie was still passed out in the aisle.

"Didn't anyone think it would be a good idea to wake her up?" he asked.

"Actually, no," said Marcus, rubbing his chest where Rosalie had given him the shove. "Marty?"

"Not me," he said.

"Oh, good heavens," said Mr. Fennelmyer. "Somebody wake her up." He unbuckled his seatbelt and got out of his seat.

"Devin, you caught the vial; it's your duty to wake her," Brac said.

Devin looked at the vial and then at Rosalie. Shrugging, he got out of his seat and knelt about two feet away from Rosalie's head keeping his distance.

"Just unplug it and put the opening under her nose?" he asked.

"Yes, said Marty, "but it has to be under her nose when you open it. The crystals inside vaporize almost instantly when they contact air."

Devin leaned forward reaching with both arms to get the vial under Rosalie's nose. He was off-balance. As he pulled the stopper out of the vial he fell forward. He managed to keep the vial by her nose for an instant before being forced to put his hands down to catch himself. He was eye-to-eye with Rosalie when her eyes popped open. Marissa grabbed his ankles and pulled him away just before Rosalie growled and tried to head-butt him.

"Ohhhh," she moaned sitting up and rubbing her forehead. "I hate magic."

Mr. Fennelmyer took one of her hands and pulled her gently to her feet. He sat her down. "I'm sorry for your headache," he said, "but this all started when you decided to show Cali some magic."

"I know," Rosalie said, tearing up. "I couldn't help it. I just wanted the new girl to like me. Everyone else hates me."

There was an awkward silence as the kids looked at each other and then at Rosalie. It was Felicia who broke the silence.

"Nobody hates you," she said. There were mumbled words of agreement from the others. "It's just that your magic, mixed with your temper, is kind of scary."

"I know," Rosalie blubbered, her tears streaming freely now. "And I've probably scared the new girl away, haven't I?" She shot Cali a quick, embarrassed, hopeful glance. Her nose was running.

All eyes on the bus turned to Cali. Cali's eyes jumped from Rosalie to Felicia and then to Shelley. She covered her face with her hands. Her thoughts and feelings were jumbled. She felt numb inside. She didn't know what to say.

"You're going to get on Bus 13 after school aren't you?" asked Veronica.

"Of course she is," said Jimmy. "Aren't you?"

There was a pause. Cali said nothing and didn't remove her hands from her face.

"We could really use someone like you," Brac said.

That brought Cali's hands down. "Like me?" she said. The edge of cynicism in her voice surprised even her. "How does someone like me fit on this bus? You're all so . . ." she searched for the word.

"Freaky?" Shelley said quietly. She spoke the word plainly, with no sense of self-pity. Still, hearing her say the word made Cali feel guilty.

Cali met Shelley's blue eyes. Her face was plain and her hair was frizzy, but in her eyes Cali saw her running like the wind over that ridge with the wolves on her heels.

"No, I didn't—" Cali began, but got no farther before Mr. Fennelmyer interrupted.

"Good heavens. Here comes Principal Kay." The other buses were pulling away. The last of the kids from those buses disappeared into the school through the gymnasium doors. "Quick, everyone, off the bus," he said, reaching over his seat and flicking the door switch. "And act normal," he added, conspiratorially.

The kids quickly gathered their things.

"And act normal?" Freddy asked, mimicking Mr. Fennelmyer, as he slung his bag over his shoulder.

"'This above all, to thine own self be true,'" responded Bric, his finger in the air.

"Polonius from *Hamlet*," Brac said. "Very good."

"Thank you," said Bric. "I thought it was appropriate."

"So do we follow Fennelmyer or Polonius?" asked Freddy.

"Actually," Felicia said, "I think both are telling us the same thing."

"Yes," said Bric. "Freak-, er," he glanced at Cali, "peculiar is normal for us."

"Would you cut the philosophy?" Mr. Fennelmyer groaned. In a half whisper he said, "Veronica, run interference."

Mr. Kay, smiling and clearly feeling much more relaxed than Mr. Fennelmyer, put his foot on the first step.

"Good morning Principal Kay," said Mr. Fennelmyer.

"Everything all right?" asked Mr. Kay. He would have climbed the steps, but Veronica adroitly got to the steps first, so he just stood by the door.

"Veronica, you're going to have a black eye," Mr. Kay said, stopping Veronica and raising her face with his fingers under her chin. "You haven't been wrestling with Arnold, have you?" He was only half teasing.

"No, just bumped it when I landed this morning," she said as she squeezed passed him on the steps.

"Landed?" Mr. Kay looked up at Mr. Fennelmyer.

"That's what she calls getting on the bus," Mr. Fennelmyer said, with only the slightest hesitation. "You know, imagination and all that."

Mr. Kay gave a troubled smile as Veronica slipped past him and skipped towards the school.

"How are Bric, Brac, Freddy?" he said to Bric, Freddy and Brac as they got off.

"I'm Freddy."

"And I'm Brac," they corrected him.

Mr. Kay laughed. "Well it's not my fault the stork got you two mixed up on delivery."

"The stork had nothing to do with it," Bric said.

"It's true," Brac added. "Babies come from eggs and sp—."

"Yes, yes," Mr. Kay interrupted. "It's just a turn of phrase."

Arnold and Miguel clambered down. "Arms *good*," Arnold said, flexing as he went past.

"Just keep them to yourself today, okay?" Mr. Kay said. "Felicia, Shelley, nice to see you."

A teacher called to him from the direction of the school. He gave Mr. Fennelmyer a wave and left.

Warren, Marissa, and Devon filed past Mr. Fennelmyer and down the steps.

"Love the hats," Mr. Fennelmyer called.

"We could get you one," said Marissa over her shoulder.

"It's okay. I'm not sure I want a tail running down my neck."

Cali stayed in her seat as the others got off. She wanted to walk to the school alone. She purposefully stared out the window as the other kids walked down the aisle. She could feel their eyes on her as they passed.

When the sounds of footsteps ended she turned to go. Rosalie stood by her seat, waiting.

"Rosalie, what are you still doing on the bus?" Mr. Fennelmyer asked.

Rosalie ignored him. "You coming?"

Cali looked down at the wet spot on her pant leg. She really wanted to walk alone.

"Come on," Rosalie said, and reached for Cali's hand.

Cali jerked her hand away.

Rosalie's eyes filled with tears.

"You are afraid of me, aren't you?" she said, one tear spilling over. "Because of me you aren't going to keep riding Bus 13." She turned and hurried up the aisle.

Kindness is never wrong, her Dad said. *Never.*

Cali stood. "Rosalie," she called.

Rosalie, stubborn and hurt, didn't stop. Mr. Fennelmyer accidentally-on-purpose stood up in her way. "I think Cali called you," he said, innocently.

Rosalie hesitated. She turned and faced Cali. The fierceness in her eyes was softened by the tears on her cheeks.

Cali, hiding her fear, held out her hand. "Could you show me the way to the office?"

A flicker of hope ran across Rosalie's face. Stubbornly she narrowed her eyes and asked, "Are you going to ride Bus 13 this afternoon?"

Cali didn't answer. She didn't know. She just stood there with her hand out and a weak smile on her face. Rosalie looked pleadingly up at Mr. Fennelmyer.

"Nobody can make someone ride Bus 13," he said. "If they did Bus 13 would cease to be."

Rosalie looked like she was going to cry again in frustration.

"Nobody can make somebody else be a friend, either," Mr. Fennelmyer went on. "So when someone offers freely. . ." he trailed off nodding toward Cali.

Rosalie's expression softened. She even smiled as she took Cali's hand. Cali looked back, "You said if I got on the bus I would find out who I am. I still don't know."

Mr. Fennelmyer looked like he was going to speak, but Rosalie pulled Cali away toward the school.

.

CHAPTER 15 – A LITTLE PRANK

Stepping off the bus was like climbing out of a swimming pool after a long swim—Cali felt heavy and sluggish. The day felt darker, like a cloud had rolled in front of the sun. Cali looked up. The sun was up and the sky was clear.

"Don't worry. You get used to it," Rosalie said.

"Used to what?"

"How it feels getting off Bus 13."

Cali glanced at Rosalie. For a fourth grader she was perceptive.

"I feel horrible," Cali said. "Does riding Bus 13 make you sick?"

"No, but getting off it does." Rosalie thought a moment. "It doesn't really make you sick. It's just that Bus 13 has so much energy. You don't notice until you get off." Rosalie gave Cali a sly glance. "You're new on the bus. If you keep riding you'll get to where you hardly notice it."

Cali looked ahead. The other kids from Bus 13 were just reaching the gymnasium doors. Jimmy, in his plaid shorts and white gym socks, had lost his classy aura. He looked dweebish now. Veronica skipped a couple of steps. The supremely confident girl who had floated through the emergency hatch on a parachute looked nothing more than the fourth grader that she was.

Cali heard the release of airbrakes behind her. At the growl of a diesel engine she turned. Mr. Fennelmyer was steering the bus toward the road. She hoped he might wave. He didn't even glance her way.

I wonder where he'll go now.

Cali felt dizzy. She brought the hand that Rosalie wasn't holding to her head. It was part of the heaviness she was feeling.

What a morning! she thought. Gas and wolves and magic. What a crazy bunch of kids! It all was just a bunch of craziness, right?

Cali looked down at Rosalie. Her brown hair danced on her shoulders as she walked. She looked up, her brown eyes happy.

"You're not really magic," Cali mumbled.

Cali hadn't meant for Rosalie to hear, but she did. Rosalie stopped Cali with a jerk of her arm. In a flash the fierceness returned to her face. "You are forgetting already, aren't you?"

"Forgetting?" Cali asked, startled.

"I know they told you," Rosalie said. "People who quit riding Bus 13 forget about Bus 13. But you haven't forgotten because you haven't decided not to ride yet, right?" Rosalie was telling, not asking.

Cali said nothing. Rosalie gave her arm another jerk. "Don't tell me you've forgotten or I'll make you remember. You know I can do it."

"I . . . I," Cali stuttered, her brain in a fog.

"I'll do it," Rosalie said. "I don't care what happens if I do."

Rosalie was short, even for a fourth grader. The warning in her voice was full size. Rosalie's threat was just enough intimidation to startle her and push some of the fog and confusion from Cali's head.

"Mr. Fennelmyer would be angry," Cali said, wishing she could say something with more leverage.

"Mr. Fennelmyer isn't here to try to stop me this time," Rosalie said.

Rosalie's response helped clear Cali's mind. They had both experienced the same Mr. Fennelmyer on the bus. The morning ride hadn't been a dream.

"Don't," Cali said. "Don't do it. I remember now. I promise you, today I won't forget."

The look of happiness on Rosalie's face was worth the promise. Not forgetting, at least for today, was the right thing.

"What, exactly, did you mean when you said, 'I don't care what happens?'" asked Cali.

Rosalie hung her head. "When you try to force people to think or feel differently than they really do it doesn't go well for them or for me. It's bad magic."

Bad magic. Cali repeated the words in her head and shivered. She was going to ask more about 'bad magic', but Rosalie was leading her around the school instead of to the gymnasium doors.

"Where are we going?"

"You want to go to the office, don't you? This way is better."

They turned in front of the building and continued toward the front doors. It became more crowded. A long line of parents in cars dropped their kids off at the curb. Principal Kay was at the front doors greeting kids by name as they came in.

"Sheri. Layden. Mark. Sulley. Rosalie."

He paused when he saw Cali. "The new girl?" he asked

"Cali McAllister," Cali said.

"Yes, yes," Principal Kay said. "Linda said your Mom registered you over the phone." He hesitated here, and then asked, "So you came with Rosalie on Bus 13?"

"She sure did," Rosalie said.

Principal Kay looked Cali up and down one more time. Cali realized he was looking for the reason she rode Bus 13. She felt offended, but just smiled.

"Good," he said a little absently. "Good. If you'll just go to the office," he indicated just inside the front doors, "Linda will take care of you."

Rosalie walked into the office holding Cali's hand. It was a brightly lit room full of hustle and bustle. The phone was ringing, kids were waiting at the counter, and teachers hurried in and out through doors in the back. Pulling Cali around the line of kids, Rosalie stepped up to the counter. An older boy started to say something, but he stopped short when Rosalie narrowed her eyes.

"Linda," she said, while Linda was still finishing up a call. Linda raised her hand for Rosalie to wait, but Rosalie went on. "This is Cali McAllister. She's the new girl."

Linda, a younger lady who looked too pretty and delicate to be a school secretary, didn't bother to chide Rosalie for interrupting her. "Good to meet you, Cali," she said as she hung up the phone. "Your mother registered you on Friday. She's a lawyer, isn't she?" She looked a little wistful for an instant. "I think you're in Mrs. Earl's class, but I need to double check."

"I was hoping she would be in my class," said Rosalie.

"She's a sixth grader. You're a fourth grader," Linda said with a calmness owned by talented people who are used to answering obvious questions all day long.

"A girl can hope," Rosalie said, hopefully.

"You get to class," Linda said. "I'll take care of Cali from here."

"You better take good care of her," Rosalie said, losing the smile and going all business. Ignoring the look of patient irritation on Linda's face, Rosalie turned to Cali and said "See you at lunch." With that she let go of Cali's hand.

Linda's phone rang again. The other kids in the line were growing impatient. "Could you sit over there and give me a minute?" Linda asked, somehow managing a genuine smile.

There was a couch against the wall. An unhappy-looking boy was sitting on it. He didn't look like he wanted to share. Cali took the chair on the other side of a potted plant, instead. It was next to a door labeled "Counselor." She heard a phone ringing in the office and then a lady's voice. Cali studied the "You can do it" and "Let's be kind" posters on the walls. She heard Shelley's name mentioned. It was whoever was on the phone in the counselor's office. She wondered if they were talking about the Bus 13 Shelley.

Cali knew better than to purposely eavesdrop on private conversations. The door was open, so how private could it be? The lady inside gave the door a shove and it swung shut, almost. It must have been a millimeter from latching before it slowly opened a crack.

". . . and she's come a long way," the lady was saying. "In fact, I don't know how much more we can expect to get out of therapy."

There was a pause as she listened.

"Not all children who have been abducted or even abused are dysfunctional for life. Many show a resiliency that is inspiring and go on to live happy and productive lives. I fully believe Shelley is one of these."

Another pause.

"No, Shelley may never be who she was before. That doesn't invalidate who she is now. She's much quieter, but she's retained a sweetness in spite of what happened. I sense a strength in her that is amazing."

Almost too late Cali realized the woman was coming to the door. She must have noticed it was still open. Cali leaned forward so she could see around the potted plant. She looked at the boy on the couch.

"So, whose class are you in?" she asked as the woman stuck her head out the door.

"Mr. Carpenter's," the boy said, turning away from her.

The counselor pulled her head back in and shut the door. As she did Cali heard her say, "Shelley should be here soon."

Cali sat feeling stunned. Shelley had been abducted? Well, of course, Shelley had told her that. Did everyone know it was by wolves? No, they couldn't know that any more than she could before she rode Bus 13. Who did they think Shelley had been abducted by? The lady had said good things about Shelley. Cali smiled. My Shelley, she thought.

"Okay, Cali," Linda said, as she hurried around the end of the counter. "It's time for you to meet your new class."

No sooner had they left the office and turned up the hallway than Cali saw Shelley coming the other way walking beside a teacher's aide. Cali hardly recognized her. It wasn't that she looked any different. She was still plain with the frizzy hair and long legs. It was the way she felt that was different. She had been quiet on the bus, but there was a sense of life about her. Now, her face was emotionless and she walked as if she wasn't entirely present.

For a moment Cali thought that Shelley was going to walk past without noticing her. Almost by accident Shelley's eyes wandered to Cali's. Their eyes met. Cali saw a blue glint. It could have just been an odd reflection from the overhead lighting. Cali knew better. On a whim Cali raised her hand in a high five. Shelley's hand came up slow, but it made it in time. Their hands met solidly with a satisfying *whap* as they passed.

Linda looked back. Then she looked down at Cali. "You know Shelley?" she asked.

"Rode the bus with her this morning," Cali said.

"You . . . you ride Bus 13?" Linda asked.

Cali nodded.

Although she tried to be discreet Cali noticed Linda's sideways glances. She could only guess that Linda was trying to figure out what it was that put her on Bus 13.

When you figure it out let me know, Cali thought.

They turned left where the hallway teed off, walked past the library, and ended up at the last classroom door. Linda didn't let Cali prepare for the awkward moment when she would step into a new class in the middle of a semester. Linda walked right in through the open door. Cali had to follow.

Only half the eyes in class turned to her when she entered, the other half were on a boy standing beside his desk. It was Freddy and he was naming the four oceans of the world.

"Pacific, Atlantic, Indian, and Arctic."

"Not bad for so early in the morning," Mrs. Earl began.

"But if you are at all progressive," Freddy interrupted, "you will agree with some scientists who count the Antarctic Ocean as the fifth ocean of the world."

Many of the kids who were watching Freddy rolled their eyes.

"I can also name the thirteen marginal seas of the Atlantic Ocean."

Several of the kids laughed. Others moaned.

Mrs. Earl, an older teacher with a pleasant face, said, "That won't be necessary, Bric. You can take your seat."

Bric? Cali looked at his shirt again. It was the brown Idaho Spuds shirt. This was Freddy.

"This must be Cali," said Mrs. Earl. "Welcome. Would you take the desk next to Bric?"

Cali had to hold her tongue to stop from correcting her. She gave Freddy a what-do-you-think-you're-doing look as she sat down.

His face blushed a little. He stared at her curiously like everyone else in class, betraying nothing.

"Perhaps you can tell us a little about yourself just so that everyone in class doesn't have to ask you individually." Mrs. Earl wore a flower-print dress and glasses with a chain so that they could hang around her neck when she didn't want to wear them. She looked old-fashioned, like Cali's Great-Aunt Elsa.

Not sure whether she was supposed to or not, Cali stood. "I'm Cali McAllister. I just moved down from Salt Lake City." She stopped and thought. There didn't seem to be anything else they needed to know, so she sat down.

"That was succinct," Mrs. Earl said. "Are you sure there's nothing else you'd like to share?"

"She's a fellow Bus Thirteener," Freddy offered loudly.

There was a soft laugh from someone in the room that cut off as quickly. What followed was a very polite silence that said, 'It's okay. We've been trained not to judge in this class.'

Cali, blushing deeply, and not fully understanding why, turned and stared at Freddy. She honestly wanted to know why he felt the class needed to know she rode Bus 13. Freddy sat doodling in his notebook as if he hadn't said anything at all. His nonchalance made her angry.

"Thank you, Freddy," she said in a calm but pointed voice just loud enough for the entire class to hear.

The class tittered. Mrs. Earl smiled. "Oh, that's not Freddy. That's Bric, although they do look a lot alike, don't they?"

Cali looked at Mrs. Earl and smiled a condescending smile that said, 'Of course you're right if you think you're right.'

The confidence faded from Mrs. Earl's face. She studied Freddy.

Freddy doodled on, cool as a cucumber, as if he wasn't aware of what Cali had done.

Oh, you're good, Cali thought.

"Let's open up to the section on the Red Sea," Mrs. Earl said, choosing not to pursue the question. "Isaac, get Cali a book, please."

Cali was now an official member of the class.

CHAPTER 16 – OUT-TRICKING A TRICKSTER

Mrs. Earl's classroom was pleasant. Big windows overlooking the playground and letting in the morning sunshine helped a lot. More than that colorful posters of exotic places and quotable quotes hung on the walls. Pictures of each class member were on the bulletin board with a list of his or her favorite things underneath. The slim, red snake flicking its tongue in the glass case with its rock and stick were a nice touch. After a half hour observing, Cali realized that it was Mrs. Earl's presence that made the room so comfortable. She appeared old-fashioned and strict, but it was clear she genuinely liked kids.

In the midst of the geography lesson centered on the Red Sea Mrs. Earl surprised Cali by calling on her.

"Cali, to which ocean is the Red Sea attached?"

Cali squirmed. She was completely unprepared for the question. Her class in Salt Lake City hadn't yet studied the Red Sea. She was startled when Freddy spoke up.

"If you need some assistance, just ask the expert."

"Bric," Mrs. Earl said. Her eyes rested on him for several seconds as if gathering her thoughts.

A master of the pause, thought Cali. Her father had pointed out how pauses have been effective in winning courtroom cases.

"I have just ascertained that Cali does not know everything."

For an uncomfortable moment Cali thought Mrs. Earl was mocking her.

"What do you think about that, class?"

The entire class yelled out, "Underwhelmed."

"Yes, it is entirely underwhelming to learn that a person doesn't know everything, unless it's you," she paused again, then said with a slight emphasis, "*Bric.*"

Cali heard a whispering sound make its way around the class.

A susurration. I just heard a susurration.

Ever since she had learned what the word 'susurration' meant she had wanted to hear the sound.

"Cali," Mrs. Earl said. "We are going to play a little game we created just for Bric. He knows an amazing number of facts. Because of this he sometimes forgets he doesn't know everything. This game helps him remember." She paused, then added, "Well, most of the time anyway."

Mrs. Earl looked at Freddy. Cali wasn't certain, but she thought she saw a friendly smile crack her rather severe-looking face.

She went on. "You may ask *Bric* questions. When you finally ask a question he can't answer we get the pleasure of hearing him stand and say, 'I don't know everything.' If you run out of questions before Bric runs out of answers, well, then, he gets to stand and take a bow."

Cali studied Freddy trying to decide whether he was taken by surprise by this game since it was meant for Bric. She couldn't tell. He sat calmly coloring in a triangle he had doodled. He glanced up at Mrs. Earl and responded to her hint of a smile with a shallow grin of his own.

Freddy's composure irritated Cali. Surely she could find a question that would stump him. *It would be for his own good,* she thought.

"The only rules are that you have to ask questions to which the answers are publicly available," said Mrs. Earl, "and, second, you can only ask questions that you know the answers to. You may begin."

That last rule made Cali hesitate. This game could quickly backfire on her. It didn't show only how much Freddy knew, but how much she knew. How quickly would she run out of questions that she knew the answers to? Looking at his smug face she knew she had to try. She started with subjects that had been recently covered in her science class.

"How far away from the sun is the earth?"

"It's ninety-three million miles." He hadn't even taken time to blink.

Cali opened her mouth to ask another question, but Freddy interrupted, "That distance is also known as one astronomical unit."

A few in the class clapped. A few others laughed at how Cali had opened her mouth to ask another question only to be cut off by Freddy's extra information. Cali blushed, but grew more determined.

"How do you calculate how much you would weigh on the moon?"

"Take your weight and divide by six," Freddy said, and yawned.

"What is the nearest galaxy to the Milky Way?"

"Andromeda," he said, sounding bored. "Ask me how far away it is."

"Foul," called out Mrs. Earl. "Why *Bric*," she said, curiously emphasizing his name, "you know that it's against the rules for you to interrupt the questions in any way. I wonder how you have forgotten that. One more infraction and you are disqualified."

Cali thought she detected a slight blush on Freddy's cheeks. Mrs. Earl nodded at her to go on.

Seeing that he had astronomy down she switched to geography.

"What is the deepest lake in the world?"

"Lake Baikal."

"What is the tallest mountain on Earth?" Cali winced at this question. It was too easy. Any first grader knew the answer.

"Mauna Kea," Freddy answered.

Cali's eyes widened in disbelief. Had he actually gotten that wrong? Everyone knew it was Mt. Everest. She looked at Mrs. Earl for confirmation.

She nodded her head, a little sadly. "It's true," she said. "We've had that question before and we've confirmed it. Mt. Everest is the tallest mountain above sea level, but Mauna Kea is the tallest in vertical feet from its base. It's about 13,000 feet tall above sea level, but another 20,000 feet lies underwater. All together it's over 33,000 feet high." Raising an eyebrow Mrs. Earl looked at Freddy and said, "*Bric's* answer is acceptable."

Cali started to feel nervous. *Did* Freddy know everything? *No, of course he doesn't*, she thought, but what was it he didn't know? Her confidence was fading. A sinking feeling in her stomach told her that she was going to run out of questions before she found out. The thought of him standing to take a bow made her fume. She had to find a way to win this.

You have to take what your opponents give you and use it against them, her father said. *Defendants who think they're smart often say too much in court.*

It was clear that Freddy, or *Bric*, was really smart. It was going to be hard to win by making him appear less than brilliant. Could she use his brilliance against him? A vague idea formed in her head. Maybe she didn't have to find what *Bric* didn't know to win; maybe she could get him with what he *did* know. It was a long shot, but if she set it up perfectly maybe there was a chance.

Quickly she asked, "What is the fastest land animal?"

"Cheetah."

"What is the largest mammal?"

"Blue Whale."

"Which is farther below sea level? Death Valley or Dead Sea?

"Dead Sea."

"Give me *pi* to the tenth decimal." She had memorized this to fifteen decimals with her dad in honor of National *Pi* Day on March 14th last year.

"3.1415926535."

"Is that right?" Mrs. Earl asked.

Cali nodded. The class cheered and clapped. Apparently this was a new question in the game.

Cali, acting flustered, narrowed her eyes like she was going to try to be really tricky. She needed to sell this for it to work. Freddy watched her with interest, glowing with confidence from his *pi* answer.

"How are your powers of observation?"

"Excellent," he answered.

"Then, quick, tell me what Bric was wearing this morning."

Freddy, hungry for more applause, answered proudly. "Blue button-up shirt with SpongeBob embroidered on the pocket."

The expected applause did not come. For the first time today Freddy looked confused.

"One of two things just happened," Mrs. Earl said, breaking the silence. "Either Cali has proven you a mere mortal by giving you a question you answered incorrectly, or you are not Bric."

Freddy looked down at his shirt and then up at Mrs. Earl. Cali could see the wheels turning fast in his head. He opened his mouth to explain, but the look on Mrs. Earl's face stopped him. Giving up he grinned sheepishly.

Turning to Cali, he said, "Well done."

The class erupted into applause.

"Way to go, Cali," one boy called out.

"Yeah, it's about time somebody put him in his place," said another.

As proud as she was for making Freddy stumble, Cali heard a mean tone to the last boy's voice. That bothered her. She looked at Freddy to see if he minded. He gave no sign.

"Hold it down," Mrs. Earl called. As the class quieted she got up and walked to the door. I'll be right outside the door, so don't try anything," she said.

She disappeared into the hallway. A second later they heard her speaking from the classroom door next to theirs. She returned with a blushing Bric.

"We just played the Question Game with you." She stopped and looked at Bric. "You lost."

"What?" He looked at Freddy. "You ruined my perfect score?"

"Not true," said Freddy. "I answered every question correctly, right Mrs. Earl?"

"That is correct. Unfortunately, Freddy's correct answers led to your being found out."

"She's tricky," Freddy said with admiration, indicating Cali with his thumb as he walked to the door.

"Oh, hi Cali," Bric said, taking his seat. "I wouldn't expect anything less from a fellow Bus Thirteener."

Someone in the room groaned, and Cali wondered why they had to publicly point that out.

CHAPTER 17 – KEEP ITS SECRETS

"Now that we have everyone where they should be, let's pair up for our civic project," Mrs. Earl said.

Cali sat feeling lost as desks turned and pushed together so that students sat face to face. Cali didn't know where she was supposed to go. She saw Bric look at her hopefully. Just before he spoke the girl across the aisle raised her hand.

"Mrs. Earl. My partner isn't here today. Could I partner with Cali?"

"That would be fine. You can catch her up," Mrs. Earl said.

Cali watched as Bric slid his desk next to two other boys' desks. Apparently there was an odd number in the class and one group had to have three in it. As smart as Bric was any group should be glad to have him, but Cali noticed the other boys treated him like a tag-a-long.

"My name's Karlyn," said the girl after they had arranged their desks. Her dark hair fell over her shoulders in a kinky waterfall. Her bright brown eyes and dimples made her plain face inviting.

"I'm Cali."

"I know," Karlyn said with a giggle. "You make quite an entrance."

Cali blushed. With the Freddy-Bric incident she certainly wasn't staying under the radar.

"No, it was great," Karlyn said. "We haven't had this much fun since I've been in this class."

"How long's that?" Cali asked.

"Only about six weeks."

"Oh," said Cali. So she wasn't the only new kid in town.

"It's hard moving in the middle of the year, isn't it? This is my third time."

"Really?" Hearing this made Cali feel bad. She had put up a fuss over this move. "Does moving so much make it easier or harder?"

"It's just as hard every time," Karlyn said. A somber look crossed her face She quickly hid it behind a smile that carried a dimple in each cheek. "There are always more interesting people to meet," she said, in imitation grownup voice. "At least that's what my mom always says."

"Your parents tell you things, too?" Cali asked.

"Mainly Mom. Dad doesn't say much to me unless I'm watching football with him." There was that smile and dimples again. "Maybe Mom's right. If we hadn't moved here I wouldn't have met you."

Karlyn's words of approval sent a thrill through Cali.

It's important to feel good about yourself, her Mom said, *but people who use flattery aren't your friends.*

Was it just flattery? Karlyn was a little too friendly.

"So you ride Bus 13?" Karlyn asked. She asked it casually enough, but the question made Cali suspicious.

"I rode it today," Cali said, cautiously.

Karlyn's brow furrowed. "You mean you don't have to ride it?"

"No." Cali thought a moment. "Actually, I don't think anyone *has* to ride Bus 13."

"Really?" Karlyn looked perplexed. "Then why did you ride it?"

Is she wondering why a normal girl like me would ride Bus 13, or is she trying to discover the freak in me that she thinks I'm hiding?

Karlyn flashed her smile and dimples in an attempt to ward off the awkwardness of her question.

Awkward or not, it was a good question. Cali thought about it. Finally she said, "The bus stopped. I got on."

"Well, they probably made a mistake," Karlyn said, taking courage that Cali hadn't gotten mad at her question. "You seem pretty normal to me."

Cali felt the thrill of those words. Was it flattery again? Or was it just true? She glanced at Bric and felt troubled. Both he and Freddy had publicly claimed her as a Bus Thirteener. That had embarrassed her. If she was 'normal' as Karlyn proclaimed then she wasn't really a Bus Thirteener. This possibility bothered her.

Who are you? Mr. Fennelmyer's words whispered in her head.

She glanced over at Bric. He slouched in his seat while the other two boys leaned in close to each other in earnest discussion. Did he know who he was? She guessed he probably did. Was he happy about who he was? At the moment he didn't look very happy.

"So, I like to watch people," Karlyn said, breaking in to Cali's thoughts, "and I've been watching the Bus 13 kids."

"Oh?" Cali said. Karlyn had her attention now.

"With all my moving around I've gotten pretty good at watching people and figuring them out." Karlyn sounded proud. "That's how I can tell you are different from the other kids on Bus 13."

"And how am I different?"

With a wave of her hand Karlyn said, "You just seem so normal."

Karlyn with the bright eyes and cute dimples says I'm normal. Being called normal wasn't the height of flattery, but Cali wasn't used to open acceptance. In her old school no one said good or bad about her. She had been invisible.

Flattery is a form of deception— started her mom.

Oh, Mom. Just let me enjoy the moment. But her Mom's words started Cali's mind whirring.

'Normal' is a synonym of 'ordinary.' 'Ordinary' is an antonym of 'extraordinary.' Karlyn's telling me I'm not extraordinary like the other kids on Bus 13. It bothered Cali that she was tempted to feel good about that.

"Something about the other kids on Bus 13 bothers me," Karlyn whispered. She shot a glance at Bric to make sure he wasn't able to hear.

"And what's that?" Cali asked, leaning closer to Karlyn.

"They seem happier than they should be."

"What does that mean?" Cali asked. "Shouldn't they be happy?"

"Well, no. I don't mean it like that," Karlyn said, frustrated as she looked for words. "What I mean is that the kids in this school don't treat them so well, but they don't seem to notice."

This still sounded mean to Cali. "So it bothers you that Bus Thirteeners are too stupid to be miserable?" This was what Cali's dad would call a leading question. It wasn't good form to ask leading questions because it was manipulative, but Cali was upset.

"Nooo," Karlyn said, her frustration growing. "They all seem too smart to not know how they're being treated. They're so happy anyway. How do they do that?"

If Karlyn was being insincere, her question meant that she was unhappy that the Bus Thirteeners weren't unhappy. Cali's intuition told her Karlyn was being sincere. That meant her question was how were the Bus Thirteeners so strong?

Intelligence is measured from the questions a person asks, not the facts that he knows. Another of her Dad's favorite quotes.

Karlyn was asking an excellent question. Cali looked at Bric. He was still being excluded from the other two boys' conversation, or maybe he just wasn't interested. Either way, he seemed at peace as he practiced his cursive writing in his notebook. He felt her gaze and looked up curiously. He grinned and went back to his writing.

"So what's it like on Bus 13?" Karlyn asked, leaning in. This wasn't an intelligent question. It was just Karlyn in *give me the gossip* mode.

Cali was disappointed. For a moment she had thought Karlyn might be extraordinary. Irritated, Cali said, "What's it like on *your* bus?"

Cali blushed as she heard the words came out of her mouth. She was acting like a four-year-old. *You're a poo poo head*, says one. *No, you're a poo poo head*, says the other.

Karlyn didn't seem to notice. "Oh, your wrestlers talking tough. Your obnoxious boys making rude noises. Your silly girls being silly. Your popular girls being boring." She wrinkled her nose on this last one. "Just the usual."

Karlyn stopped and looked at Cali expectantly. It was Cali's turn.

"What's it like on Bus 13?" How do you tell someone what it's like on Bus 13? On a whim she told it straight. "Well, today Warren dropped his marbles and got dragged off by the wolves. Veronica actually parachuted in through the emergency hatch. And did you know that Rosalie can light her fingers like candles?"

Karlyn sat frozen, her brown eyes wide, her jaw slowly dropping.

A panic squirmed to life in the pit of Cali's stomach. She had supposed that her words were so outrageous in spite of their truth that Karlyn wouldn't take them seriously even for a second. Karlyn was weighing Cali's words as if they could be true. Cali realized she had broken an unwritten law—you don't speak of what happens on Bus 13.

In books people who abuse magic lose the magic. Something told her that her right to ride Bus 13, or the existence of Bus 13 itself, was on the line. She may not have decided to keep riding Bus 13, but . . . .

It's not my fault. No one told me the rules, she thought.

Ignorance is not a valid defense, her dad said. *You break the law, you pay the penalty.*

Cali watched Karlyn digest what she had just heard. There was a look of amazement on her face—the look of a person believing the unbelievable.

"Oh, really," Cali said, chuckling, "you are too funny the way you can play along."

She saw disappointment in Karlyn's eyes and actually felt it when it reached her heart. Cali felt it so keenly that she brought her hand to her chest.

Karlyn hoped it could be true, Cali realized. *I just broke her heart with a lie.*

"Oh, Cali," Karlyn said, working hard to hide the disappointment. "I can't believe I almost believed you."

Had Cali lied well enough? Or had she severed her tie to Bus 13? She looked at Bric hoping for a sign. He was busy seeing how high the spring-loaded clicker at the end of his pen could shoot it into the air.

"Bric," she said. He didn't look. "Bric," she said again. There was a tinge of panic in her voice.

This time he looked, but there was no sign of recognition.

She wanted to reach over, grab his embroidered SpongeBob shirt, and shake him. *You remember me. You do.* Instead, she lifted her arm in the air and gave the closed fist solidarity salute. "SpongeBob, forever," she said just loud enough for him to hear.

His eyes lit up. The most beautiful smile she had ever seen graced his face—he knew her. He lifted his arm in the same salute. "SpongeBob," he said, louder than he should have.

"I don't know what world you're living in, Bric," Mrs. Earl said from the back corner where she was helping two girls, "but please come back to this one."

Bric's partners rolled their eyes, and other kids laughed; Bric's smile never wavered.

Turning back to Karlyn, who was watching closely, Cali said dismissively, "That's basically what it's like on Bus 13."

"Pretty nerdy place, huh?" said Karlyn, nodding as if that's what she expected. Still, there was a little suspicion in her eyes.

"Nerd central," answered Cali.

"*You* don't seem too nerdy," Karlyn said.

"No. You're right. I'm not like the rest," Cali answered. This truth didn't make her feel good this time. Why had Bus 13 stopped for her? She was relieved that perhaps its doors weren't shut to her, yet.

Chapter 18 – Oranges and Fish and Bumps and Bruises

Midmorning the kids started closing their books and putting their desks back in rows.

"Morning recess," Karlyn said.

Mrs. Earl started making her way back to her desk. "Okay," was all she said.

That was the permission the class had been waiting for. They all got up and formed a herd at the back of the room. Some reached into coat pockets, others into their cubbies, and pulled out snacks. Most of the snacks were finger foods Moms had put in plastic sandwich bags like trail mix or pretzels. A few had carrot sticks or grapes.

Snack time? Cali wasn't prepared. She stood to one side and waited, feeling a little self-conscious. She noticed Karlyn didn't have a snack either.

"Mom gave me an orange," Karlyn said sulkily, coming over to Cali. "It's embarrassing."

"I love oranges," Cali said, "if they're sweet."

"You do?" Karlyn brightened up. She went to her coat and pulled the orange out of the pocket. "You want half of it?" She looked hopeful.

"Okay."

Karlyn held the orange up and stared at it. Cali stared at it, too. It looked like a good orange. What was Karlyn waiting for?

"Um, I hate biting them," Karlyn said. "Will you bite it?" She blushed.

Cali took it and bit it. She didn't mind the bitter taste of the peel on her front teeth. Karlyn made short work of peeling it. She pulled the orange apart and gave Cali one section more than half.

Kids milled around eating and talking. Bric was eating fish crackers. They were golden and cheesy looking. Cali thought they would taste good with the orange.

As if reading her mind Bric came over and held the bag out.

"Cracker?" he asked.

Cali took a few and laid them on an orange slice.

"Over 30,000 species of fish in the sea and I only like to eat the ones that taste like cheddar cheese," Bric said.

"Would SpongeBob approve?" asked a nearby boy.

"He loves cheesy crackers," Bric answered, authoritatively.

Another boy joined in, speaking to Cali. "That was so cool how you caught Bric this morning."

Cali tried to suppress a smile, not knowing how Bric felt about this.

"They always get away with those stunts," the boy added, a touch sulkily.

"She caught Freddy, not me," Bric said.

"Same difference," said the boy. He was eating a Snickers bar.

"Your Mom gave you that for snack time, Mike?" Karlyn asked, interrupting.

Mike hesitated, then said, "Yes."

Karlyn gave him her *You lie* look. He grinned, looking away.

"She would never have caught me. I'm smarter than Freddy," Bric went on.

"You two are just alike," said Mike, with chocolate-covered teeth.

"How do you know you're talking to Bric right now?" asked Bric.

"Your shirt," said Mike. The boy next to him nodded as he crunched a pretzel.

"It's not like we don't know how to swap shirts." Bric nonchalantly turned and walked away.

Mike and his friend stopped chewing and watched him go. Karlyn looked unsure, too. Cali would have been unsure, but she caught the wink as he turned. It was Bric all right.

A bell rang and the kids grabbed their coats and pushed their way out the door. Cali floated down the hall with the flow of kids like a fallen leaf in a brook. Ahead the brook abruptly turned a corner toward the exit.

Just before she reached the corner, Cali saw Veronica further up the hall walking next to a teacher. Veronica was anxiously looking back over her shoulder. She spotted Cali and stopped. Frantically she motioned her to come. Confused, Cali stopped so suddenly that kids knocked into her from behind.

Seeing Cali's hesitation Veronica motioned even more frantically. The teacher took a few steps before realizing Veronica wasn't at his side. He came back, looked for who Veronica was motioning to, then put a hand on Veronica's back and urged her along. Cali had temporarily looked away to avoid the notice of the teacher.

The kids from many classes flowed around her as she went from a leaf to a rock in the brook. Veronica seemed to think she needed Cali's help. Cali couldn't think of a single reason why. Veronica had taken a liking to her on the bus. Was this just some silly dramatics?

As Cali turned toward the exit Veronica threw her one last desperate glance. It was such a genuine look of desperation that Cali stopped again.

What could it be? She thought. Was she being taken to the principal? There was nothing that Cali could do to help her with that.

There was an *oof* as a body smaller than hers collided with her from behind. She turned to see Marissa in her coonskin hat looking up at her.

"Sorry. *They* pushed me," she said, looking at a pair of passing boys, her eyes daring them to do it again. Looking up she saw the indecision on Cali's face. "What's wrong?"

They hadn't even spoken to each other on the bus. Still, even a small amount of time on Bus 13 does something to you. Instead of shrugging her shoulders and saying "Oh, nothing," she blurted out, "Veronica was waving to me for help as she went into the office."

"What are you waiting for, then? Go help her," Marissa said. She spoke as if it were simple like, *if you have a rock in your shoe, stop and take it out.*

"If Veronica's gotten herself into trouble, it's her problem, not mine," she said., irritably.

Marissa, on her way to the exit doors, stopped and whipped her head around so fast that the raccoon tail slapped her in the face. In a fierce voice she said, "Warren got himself into trouble this morning and you risked your life to save him."

Her meaning was clear. If you would help Warren out of dangerous trouble, why wouldn't you help Veronica in regular school trouble?

Marissa looked thoughtful. "I never thanked you for saving Warren." She made sure Cali was looking her in the eyes before she went on. "Thanks." She turned and pushed her way out the door.

"I didn't go after Warren on purpose," Cali yelled as the door shut. Why couldn't they see that Shelly had set her up to look brave? She wasn't brave. She was a loner who didn't get involved in other people's lives. *They have no right to expect these things of me.* She had every intention of following Marissa; instead she passed the exit on her way to the office.

"Dang me," she said, disgusted with herself.

A teacher was coming up the hall from the other direction. She half expected him to stop her and ask her why she wasn't out on the playground. He only glanced at her and nodded as he passed by.

Her heart pounded harder as she reached the windows just before the open office door. Linda was sitting behind the counter gazing into a computer screen. There was no one else to be seen. Veronica must already be in the principal's office. Another reason to turn around and go to recess. Without stopping to prepare—she didn't have any ideas anyway—she strode into the office as if she owned the place, spread her arms, and said, "Ta daaa."

Fake it 'til you make it, her father always said about doing hard things. That's how he got through his first year of law school.

To her surprise Linda looked up and laughed. "Most kids aren't as happy to be seen as you are, especially here," she said, catching her breath. "What can I do for you?"

Cali panicked. She hadn't planned to act when she ent
office. She didn't even know she could act. She was just m
Cary Grant's style in *My Girl Friday*, one of her Dad's favorite movies.
Stepping up to the counter Cali leaned forward and said, "To tell you
the truth, lady, I don't have a clue."

Cali didn't know where the boldness was coming from, but it was
over now. With Linda's next question, she would turn and run.

Linda, delighted by Cali's unexpected parody, laughed again. "You
are too much," she said. "Did you just come down here to entertain
me or is there—"

Cali was ready to wave and run when the counselor's door
opened. An anxious voice could be heard mid-sentence. "—nica,
please, sit down."

Cali turned to see Veronica hanging onto the door handle. The
teacher who had brought her to the office was holding her by the wrist.
Veronica saw Cali and burst into tears. "I knew you'd come," she said
yanking her arm free from the teacher and running to Cali. "Tell them,
Cali. They won't believe me."

The counselor, a rather formidable-looking middle-aged woman
appeared at the door. "Veronica, this is none of her business."

"No, it's my business and none of yours," Veronica said, angrily.
This much boldness from such a little gal was surprising.

It's her red hair, Cali thought.

"Cali will tell you," Veronica said again. Veronica moved behind
her, partly for protection and partly to push Cali forward.

"Tell her what?" Cali asked. *What have I stepped into?*

The counselor took notice of Cali, then, and regarded her
thoughtfully. "You don't know what this is about?"

"No," Cali said, more forcefully than she meant.

"Very well. Would you come in?" she asked, stepping aside.
Looking at Veronica and raising an eyebrow she said, "And will you
please wait here with Mrs. Bringhurst?"

"Sure," Veronica said, wiping her nose with her hand. "Linda
minds her own business, don't you, Linda?"

"Oh, I'm sure I don't have any idea what goes on around here,"
Linda mumbled, forcing a smile.

Cali looked over her shoulder as she followed the counselor into the office. Veronica gave her a desperate look. She pointed to her eye and then raised her arms and squatted down quickly as if she were falling. She stood up quickly when the counselor turned to close the door.

The latch clicked and Cali felt panic in her chest. It was her first day at a new school. *Just lay low*, she had told herself. *You'll be your usual invisible self.* She hadn't counted on Bus 13 throwing her life a curve ball.

"Have a seat," the counselor said. She indicated a rather plush-looking chair in front of her desk. The counselor, a broad, strong-looking woman, went behind her desk and sat. The chair creaked loudly like something from a haunted house. The rest of her office wasn't plush. It looked kid-unfriendly. There were no posters of happy sayings, no candy jars, and no family pictures. There were shelves of brown books, a vase of plastic flowers on a side table, and bronzed diplomas hanging on the walls.

The only thing that suggested the counselor had anything to do with children was a very large and soft-looking stuffed bear sitting in a smaller chair beside the desk.

"That's Poochie Bear," said the counselor when she saw Cali looking. "I've had him ever since I was a little girl. He's a great listener and he never tells anyone's secrets. And you know what else?"

She paused. When Cali realized she was expecting an answer she shook her head.

"He's an excellent cuddler." She glanced at the bear, smiling proudly. "You can sit with him if you feel the need." She looked at Cali, encouragingly.

"Um, no, thank you," said Cali. "I'm not in the need of cuddles at the moment."

The counselor sighed, looking disappointed. "None of us realize how much more cuddling we need in our lives."

Cali blushed as she tried to imagine the big, strong-looking woman in a cuddling situation.

Leaving the subject of Poochie Bear, the counselor sat up straighter and said, "I'm Dr. Stedwell."

"You're a doctor?" Cali asked. Her last school had only had a school nurse who wasn't really even a full nurse.

"PhD," she said rather dryly, like one who had explained this too many times.

Oh, that kind of doctor, Cali thought.

Some kinds of doctors are more useful than other kinds of doctors, her dad often said, teasing her mom.

Her mom was thinking of getting a PhD, or at least she had been thinking about it before they moved. Since they made the decision to move Mom's favorite quote was, *live more simply.*

"I don't believe I know you," Dr. Stedwell said.

Who are you? Cali heard Mr. Fennelmyer's voice.

"I don't know, either," Cali said.

"Excuse me?" Dr. Stedwell said, raising her eyebrows.

"Oh, I'm Cali McAllister," Cali said, coming out of her reverie. "This is my first day. I met Veronica on the bus this morning."

"They put you on Bus 13?" Dr. Stedwell asked, eyeing her over.

Cali was getting tired of this question. "Nobody put me on Bus 13," she said, impatiently. "It stopped. I got on."

Dr. Stedwell nodded understandingly. "There is another bus that runs the same route, you know," she said. "You might consider it."

Abruptly changing the subject, Dr. Stedwell said, "I'm supposed to be speaking with Veronica right now, and yet here you are. I'm wondering why."

"I'm wondering, too," Cali said, meekly.

"Veronica seems to think that you can answer a serious question that has arisen."

Cali waited to hear the question, but Dr. Stedwell was already waiting for the answer. "Um, what's the question?" Cali asked after several seconds of silence.

"If you don't already know, I can't tell you due to the privacy of the issue." Dr. Stedwell thought for a moment before an idea occurred to her. "However, I could ask you if anything happened on the bus this morning."

What happened on the bus this morning? We had green explosions in the back of the bus. There were wolves, and a very fine rendition of Bach's *Toccata and Fugue in D Minor.* And you should have seen the expert way little Veronica parachuted into the bus.

Cali was very careful not to say these things out loud. She had learned her lesson that what happens on Bus 13 stays on Bus 13.

With a small smile she remembered her first sight of Veronica as she dropped through the hatch. It would have been perfect if Mr. Fennelmyer stopped the bus in time.

Cali's heart skipped a beat. *They've found out about Veronica parachuting to the bus!*

Dr. Stedwell saw the look of fear in Cali's eyes and leaned forward in anticipation.

Something about her conclusion didn't seem right. Would Dr. Stedwell have taken time to talk with Cali if she was certain Veronica was doing something so dangerous? And what was Veronica trying to tell her before she came into the office? It was about her black eye, that was obvious enough, but the dropping to the ground? Was that about coming down in a parachute? Or was it—*falling*?

Duh, Cali thought. *Sharp as marbles, today.* Her dad often said this when he missed the obvious.

Veronica wants me to tell them how she got her black eye—by falling down.

It occurred to Cali that this explanation was almost true, except she was actually falling up.

Cali almost betrayed a smile when she figured this out, but something else bothered her. Why were they so interested in Veronica's black eye? Kids got bumps and scrapes all the time. When did that kind of thing get the counselor's attention?

Then Cali understood. The teacher and counselor believed that someone in Veronica's home had hit her. They suspected child abuse. Cali's dad had represented a father who had been accused of child abuse. The story was in the paper. Cali's dad had believed the man's account of how the child had gotten his foot caught in the chair when he had fallen. With her dad's help the man had been exonerated, but not before his life had been almost ruined.

Cali thought fast. She had to convince Dr. Stedwell that Veronica's black eye wasn't child abuse, but she couldn't just tell her the truth, either.

Yep, Veronica came right down through the emergency hatch but Mr. Fennelmyer didn't stop the bus on time. That just wouldn't work. Cali also realized that the more eager she looked to clear Veronica, the less believable she would be. She had to work the story slowly.

"What happened on the bus?" Cali said, acting like she was trying to remember. "Well, it was pretty quiet except that Bric, Brac, and Freddy were arguing about SpongeBob."

"SpongeBob? Really?" asked Dr. Stedwell.

"Uh huh. Bric was right, of course. SpongeBob wouldn't be funny if he didn't look like a kitchen sponge." Cali could see impatience growing in Dr. Stedwell.

"Anything else?" Dr. Stedwell asked. "Maybe something to do with Veronica?"

Bingo! Now that Dr. Stedwell had brought it up she could talk about Veronica without seeming overeager. "Veronica? Let's see. No, nothing I can think of. Well, she did trip on the steps getting on the bus. She hit her head on the dash and fell into the garbage can. It was pretty funny."

Cali wasn't used to lying. Her words sounded flat and unconvincing, even to herself.

Great liars are half convinced their lies are true, her mother said. *It's bad mental health.*

Dr. Stedwell didn't look fully convinced, either. "Could Veronica already have had this bump when she got on the bus?"

"No," Cali said, "She sat down right next to me. There was nothing on her face but a little red mark where she hit the dash. I watched the bruise form as we drove to school. I told her she was going to have a shiner."

Dr. Stedwell sat back in her chair. Her face grew softer as she thought. She looked genuinely concerned about the issue. "Very well," she said. "You've been very helpful. Veronica told me she fell, but we just needed to make sure. She didn't mention the garbage can, though."

Cali laughed. "Why would anyone admit to tripping into a garbage can? That's so embarrassing." She knew.

"I suppose you're right. You may go now."

Cali was only too happy to leave the office. She was opening the door when Dr. Stedwell said, "And don't forget, you can catch the other bus."

Veronica was sitting in the chair just outside the door. She looked up, worry in her eyes.

"I just told Dr. Stedwell about your dramatic entrance onto the bus this morning," Cali said.

Veronica looked alarmed.

"You tripping and falling into the garbage can was so funny." Cali gave a convincing laugh. Veronica looked confused, but then the light turned on and she got it.

"I didn't think it was so funny," she said, smiling sheepishly.

Cali looked through the hallway window and Veronica gave her a scrunched-cheek wink as she followed Mrs. Stedwell into her office. It was going to be okay.

CHAPTER 19 – FITTING IN, OR NOT

"Cali, wait."

It was Veronica. Ignoring the 'No running in the halls' rule, Veronica came flying up the hallway. Her short legs were pumping furiously. She pulled up beside Cali, bright-eyed and breathing hard.

"Thanks!" she said between breaths. "My dad would have beat me if the child protection people accused him of beating me again."

Cali looked at Veronica in disbelief.

Veronica saw the look on her face and laughed. "That's what he tells me. He's a real crack up. Truth is he wouldn't kick a dog if it peed on his leg."

As they turned the corner Cali glanced at Veronica and wrinkled her nose.

"It's true. I've seen it happen."

Cali's laughed. "But what will he say when he sees your eye?" she asked as she pushed the door open.

Veronica made her voice deep and did her best 'dad' walk. "Be more careful next time." The morning sunlight landed on Veronica's curly red hair and freckles, lighting her up like a candle flame.

No doubt about it, Cali thought. *Veronica is one unique girl.*

Now that she was on the playground, Cali didn't know what to do. Boys and girls played basketball out on the asphalt. There was some jump roping and a fair amount of simple chasing around. Nearby, kids kicked rubber balls against the red brick walls. Beyond the asphalt was grass. Some kids threw a football clumsily back and forth. Another group chased a soccer ball. Off to the side she recognized Warren in his coonskin hat. He was on his knees with a couple of his friends playing marbles.

Cali meandered among the groups, interested enough to watch, but not enough to want to join. Veronica tagged along with her.

"What do you usually do at recess?"

"Lately I've been playing Killer Uno in the gym," Veronica said.

"They let you stay inside at recess?"

"Yep."

"Don't let me keep you," Cali said.

"It's okay," Veronica said, happily. "I need to get out more."

Says the girl who floats down out of the sky every morning, thought Cali.

Cali heard someone calling her from across the playground. She turned to see Karlyn running over. "Cali, come on. They want to meet you."

"Who does?"

"My friends." She pointed to a gaggle of girls at the edge of the blacktop near the grass. Two of the girls were especially pretty with long straight hair and delicate noses. They were already wearing makeup. They and three others were in a huddle taking turns looking in her direction. Clearly she was the current topic of conversation.

"They want to meet me?" Cali asked.

"Yes. Everyone's already heard about you and your contest with Freddy," Karlyn said, excitedly. "They heard you rode Bus 13, but I told them you were definitely different from the rest. They really want to meet you."

For the second time that day she felt the thrill of flattery.

Flattery is just an insincere way of getting something from some— began her dad.

Dad, I know, she said. *But surely enjoying the thrill for a few minutes won't hurt.*

"I'm talking to Veronica," Cali said, putting up a feeble fight against the thrill.

134

Karlyn turned and looked at Veronica as if noticing her for the first time.

"What is she, a third grader?" Karlyn asked.

"I'm fourth," Veronica said, a little too loudly.

"I'm sure she has her own little friends to play with," Karlyn said, taking Cali's arm and pulling her toward the group of girls. "You have to be careful with the little kids. You give them a minute and they'll take an hour."

Cali gave Veronica a *What can I do?* look of apology as Karlyn pulled her away.

"Cali," Veronica had equal parts hurt and pleading in her voice. "You don't want to talk to *them*."

Cali heard Veronica, but didn't look back. *Why not talk to them? They are people, too. And they want to talk to me,* Cali thought.

Flattery is just a way— her dad began again.

Shut up, Dad.

"This is Cali," said Karlyn. The circle of girls opened up and formed a half circle around Cali and Karlyn.

"So, you're new here," said the girl with the long blond hair, stating the obvious.

"Not as new as I was two and a half hours ago," said Cali.

Karlyn laughed. The other girls stared at her blank-faced. Either they didn't have a sense of humor or they just didn't get it. Cali decided on the latter. Actually, Cali was certain two of the girls in the group, the one with the freckles, and the one with the delicate little scar above her eyebrow, wanted to laugh, but didn't when the others didn't. Karlyn's laugh trailed off awkwardly in the silence.

"We heard that you are smarter than Freddy and Bric," said the blond. Oh, she was pretty. Her hair practically shone like an incandescent bulb in the light and her teeth were white and perfectly straight.

Cali was about to explain that she didn't think she was as smart as Freddy and Bric. She was going to tell them how Freddy had answered every question she could think of and that she had gotten lucky in tricking him, but Karlyn jumped in before she could begin.

"You should have heard her. I bet she's the smartest kid in the school."

Karlyn's eagerness to show off Cali to these girls was embarrassing.

"You don't look like you would be the smart type," said the blonde.

The other girls giggled. Cali blushed. Then she blushed more, embarrassed that she had blushed. As a loner she had learned a long time ago to hide signs of vulnerability.

"What Stacy means," said the brunette, "is that you look more the pretty type than the smart type."

Pretty type? Had the brunette just called her pretty? The very thought sent a flutter through her chest. She looked into the brunette's eyes. They were as dark a brown as the expensive 70% cacao bars that her mom bought.

Flattery is— her dad began.

Dad! I know what flattery is, Cali thought, but she thought she saw sincerity in the girl's eyes. *She doesn't have to be insincere just because she's pretty . . . or says that I am.*

Cali thought back to the image she saw in the mirror that morning as she walked by on her way to catch the bus. She had looked just a little pretty, hadn't she? Her hair was cut short just below her ears, but the boyish cut brought out the female charm in her face. That's what the stylist had said. Her mom had agreed.

"Thank you," Cali said, earnestly, stopping just short of gushing.

Whoa, there, she thought. *Get control of the horse. A few kindish words from popular girls and you melt into putty?*

Even after calling herself on their flattery, Cali couldn't stop the fluttering in her chest. Struggling to come back to her senses she said, "Anyway, it's not like pretty girls can't be smart, too, right? I mean, my mom is beautiful, and she's a lawyer."

The other girls shifted uncomfortably. It was like they didn't realize Cali was trying to give them a compliment.

"Your mom's a lawyer? For reals?" asked Stacy.

Cali nodded.

"Well, Brittan's mom," she motioned to the brunette, "is a secretary—"

"Administrative assistant," interrupted Brittan.

"—administrative assistant to the lawyer's office in town. But *she* won first runner up in the Miss Utah pageant ten years ago."

"Wow, that's great," said Cali. The fluttering in her chest slowed as she realized she had just lost some sort of contest.

The yells of boys behind them caught their attention. They all turned to see boys racing along the edge of the grass field. Six of them sprinted by the girls near enough that Cali felt the air turbulence their passing bodies created. A few of the girls bounced in excitement as they watched two boys take the lead and fight to cross the finish line first.

"Zack won," said Karlyn excitedly.

"Of course," said Stacy. "He's the fastest boy in the school."

"And he's your boyfriend," said Brittan.

"He is not. I don't even like him," answered Stacy unconvincingly.

"I wonder who the fastest girl is," Cali said. She asked because she had just spotted Shelley walking alone along the chain link fence on the far side of the field. Cali couldn't help seeing the image of Shelley flying smoothly over the ridge with the pack of wolves on her heels.

"Who cares?" said Stacy. The boys, breathing hard, walked by on their way back to the starting line.

"Wouldn't it be cool if the fastest girl could beat the fastest boy in the school?" said Cali.

Cali knew before she said this that it wasn't the right thing to say if she wanted to get on in this group, but, being a loner, she wasn't practiced on holding back on who she was.

"Why would that be cool?" asked Stacy, not taking her eyes off Zack.

"Do you think there's a girl in school who could actually beat Zack?" asked the girl with the scar over her eyebrow. "Do you race? I mean, are you as fast as you are smart?"

This misperception of how smart she was bothered Cali. *If they only knew how average I really am they wouldn't even be talking to me right now.*

"No, I'm not fast, but Shelley is."

The girls turned and looked at her. Even Stacy pulled her eyes off Zack. It was like they were trying to understand what she said.

"Shelley?" said Brittan. She turned toward the field and pointed. "You mean *that* Shelley?"

"Yes," Cali said. "Um, I saw her run to the bus this morning and she was fast. Really fast."

"Shelley?" said Stacy.

"Yes, Shelley," said Cali.

"It's seems to me if you put Shelley at a starting line she wouldn't be able to find the finish line, let alone win the race," said Stacy.

The girls giggled.

Karlyn smiled, but didn't giggle.

"She's never seemed all the way here since—," she hesitated, 'you know, since she went missing." There was just a touch of empathy in her voice behind the gossipy tone. "Oh, but you wouldn't know. You're new here."

"Actually, I heard about it on the bus this morning," Cali said.

Momentarily forgetting about Shelley, the girls looked at Cali with new interest.

"That's right," Brittan said. "You rode Bus 13." She laughed as if the image of Cali on Bus 13 was hilarious. "How was that?"

The memory of the crazy morning events left no room for milder things like embarrassment. "Let's just say I'll never forget it," Cali said.

The girls laughed. They laughed for all the wrong reasons, but in their laughter Cali felt the thrill of acceptance.

Cali's moment of acceptance would have been longer if the boys hadn't come racing by again. The girls turned to watch Zack once again beat the other boys. The losing boys didn't seem to mind. They gathered round Zack and cheered. Zack was loving it. He stood noticeably straighter and swaggered a little as he passed the girls.

Zack glanced at Stacy as he passed. She blushed, her face so red it looked like a cherry against her glowing, blond hair. "If I was faster than Zack I'd let him win anyway," she sighed.

Women are women and should never try to be men, but a woman should never be less than the woman she can be, her mom said.

"Shelley can beat him."

The girls turned and looked at Cali. They weren't hostile, just confused, like they didn't understand the words that were coming out of her mouth.

"You really think she can?" asked the girl with the scar.

"I know she can."

"Even if she could beat him—and I don't think she can—why would she even want to race him?" asked Stacy.

Brittan was enjoying her friend's troubled reaction to what Cali said. She stood looking at Stacy with just a hint of a grin.

"You think she would want to race Zack?" Stacy said, turning on Brittan.

"Um, maybe," she said, caught off guard. Then, remembering her place, "No. Why would she want to race Zack?" Brittan knew how to fit in.

"She might think it would be fun," Cali said.

"Maybe she would," said Stacy, "until she lost. Then she would probably cry and embarrass all of us."

"She's not the crying sort," Cali said, bluntly.

The girl with the scar, thin, but bouncy, said, "I'll go ask Zack if he'll race her." She turned and was off. Karlyn hesitated half a second to glance at Stacy and Brittan and then ran after her.

"Mindy. Karlyn. No," Stacy called, too late. She sounded put out.

Mindy didn't slow down. Karlyn slowed to a walk and almost turned around at Stacy's call, but then sped back up to a trot to catch Mindy.

Good girl, Karlyn, Cali thought. Karlyn had probably kept going only because she wanted an excuse to be near Zack, but still, Cali was starting to like the girl.

Zack looked her way as the girls talked to him. Then they turned and looked across the field at Shelley. She appeared to be lost in a daydream, meandering aimlessly.

Cali had to admit that their teasing about Shelley finding the finish line was not without reason. She didn't look to be all the way in this world. Cali started to feel a little nervous about what she had started. She hadn't really expected there to be a race, but Mindy and Karlyn ran off before she could say anything.

When Mindy and Karlyn started running toward Shelley butterflies really started fluttering in Cali's stomach. Maybe Shelley wouldn't want to race, like Stacy said.

Shelley looked up rather slowly when Mindy and Karlyn reached her. She gazed toward Zack as they spoke. She looked confused, but started walking their way.

The girls babbled in excitement and ran over to where Zack and the other boys stood.

"Are you really going to race her?" Stacy asked in disbelief.

"Well, if she thinks she's faster than me I need to teach her something," Zack said.

"She doesn't think—" Cali began, wanting to explain that Shelley had nothing to do with this, but Brittan spoke over her.

"It's hard to believe she would even dare race you," she gushed.

Cali wanted to go talk to Shelley before the race, but Zack wasted no time.

"Are you ready to go?" Zack asked as soon as Shelley arrived.

Shelley looked at Cali, her eyes still showing confusion. Then she looked at Stacy and Brittan, and finally at Zack. She nodded.

"Okay, we race to that dead spot in the grass down there between where Jace and Kayden are standing. Tyler, you start us."

Zack crouched into his starting stance. Shelley stepped up beside Zack looking casual. Cali wanted to stop the whole thing. Something about this race wasn't right, but the excitement in the air was electric and she couldn't open her mouth.

"Ready? Set." There was a pause. "Go!"

Zack took off pumping his legs so fast that he almost stumbled over his own feet just ten paces in. He recovered and flew towards the finish line.

Cali was relieved to see Shelley begin running on 'Go!', but quickly saw this wasn't going to end well. Shelley jogged along as if she were out for a leisurely morning run. Cali saw elements of Shelley's smooth running style as she jogged along, but there was none of the speed she had witnessed that morning. The butterflies in her chest dropped in her stomach like pebbles.

The kids were laughing before the race was over. Shelley had only reached the halfway point by the time Zack crossed the finish line. He started walking back toward the kids at the starting line before Shelley finished the race. He gave her a look of contempt as she jogged by him.

Stacy gave Cali a triumphant 'I told you so' look before leading the girls in a kind of celebratory bouncing circle around Zack as he neared. Some of the boys joined the circle.

"If they knew they were going to beat her, why are they so excited?" Cali said to no one in particular.

"I know, right?" said a voice behind her. "Those girls are making it hard for women like us to be taken seriously."

Cali whirled to see Veronica standing there with her hands in her pockets. Cali was crestfallen at Shelley's defeat. She wanted to run to Veronica and bury her face in her shoulder.

"Why didn't she run?" Cali asked.

Veronica shrugged. "She did," she said.

"No," Cali said, annoyed at Veronica's flippant manner. "Why didn't Shelley *really* run?"

"She can run faster than that?" Veronica asked.

Cali stared at Veronica. Did she really not know? Cali realized that Veronica hadn't actually seen Shelley run this morning. Maybe she never had.

"Veronica, the wolves chased her for miles this morning, and they couldn't catch her."

"Oh," Veronica said. She accepted this much more easily than Cali would have if Cali hadn't seen. "Then, maybe she just wasn't motivated," Veronica said. "Those wolves probably made a difference."

Shelley came walking around the crowd of kids still encircling Zack. She was back to her leisurely pace. She looked at the bouncing group of kids and smiled as if she were happy about whatever they were happy about.

"They're having fun," Shelley said as she reached Cali and Veronica.

"Yes," Cali said, lifelessly.

"Zack wanted to run with me," she said.

"Run? It was a race," Cali said.

"A race? Oh," she said. "I wondered why he started so fast. I'm pretty sure he couldn't run very far at that pace. Well, I'm glad he won."

"Why?" Cali asked, exasperated, as she watched the kids celebrate. It looked like they were just bouncing to bounce, now.

"It made them happy," Shelley said, admiring the cheering kids.

You've been around Felicia too long, Cali muttered.

Two bells rang out one after the other.

"Recess is over," Veronica said, as if stating a sad fact. Together the three of them walked slowly toward the school.

CHAPTER 20 – BEHOLD THE POWER!

Cali sat in class smarting about Shelley's loss to Zack..

What does it matter if Shelley wins a race or not? she wondered. *Oh yeah, maybe because I practically announced to the whole school that Shelley would win. It made me look stupid.*

It was embarrassing, to be sure, but something else bothered her even more. What she had witnessed that morning—Shelley outracing a pack of wolves, a pipe organ on the bus, a child parachuting through the emergency hatch—as each hour passed at school, the more dreamlike and unreal the morning events became.

"Bric," she half-whispered. During open discovery time the class was encouraged to discuss current events or other study topics. They could communicate to each other as long as they kept it to a "gentle roar," as Mrs. Earl put it. "Do you know how fast Shelley is?"

Bric, concentrating on folding a shape with a square of notebook paper, didn't look over. "Brac got a radar gun for his birthday last year, but we've never used it on Shelley."

"Wasn't Brac's birthday also your birthday?" Cali asked.

"Yes, but *I* didn't get a radar gun," he said, betraying some annoyance at that fact.

"Never mind that," Cali said, getting back on topic, "That's not what I meant. I mean have you ever just seen how fast she can run?"

"No," he said, flattening the paper into an odd diamond shape after a complex series of folds. "I did it," he said, looking surprised. He looked over at Cali to see if she saw.

"What's it supposed to be?"

"Nothing yet. It's just an advanced origami fold on the way to birthing a paper crane. Brac makes it look so easy. Twerp."

Cali sat back and gave up on the original question. Here in class she couldn't explain what she meant, anyway. Had she and Shelley really run with the wolves this morning?

Once more, without looking her way, Bric spoke. His voice was so soft she almost didn't realize he was talking to her. "Shelley's a bit of a mystery even on Bus 13. After this morning you probably know her better than the rest of us."

His words brought her relief. Her run with Shelley and the wolves had happened.

"Her eyes," he added, quietly, "aren't they amazing?"

Cali came frighteningly close to wanting to hug him. She wasn't sure why. Maybe it was because he confirmed she wasn't going crazy.

"Her eyes are pretty, aren't they?" said a voice from across the other aisle.

Cali jumped. It was Karlyn. How much had she heard? She had been discussing episodes of *Walking Dead* with Skyler.

"You're talking about Shelley's eyes, right?"

Cali nodded.

"No one has eyes like her. Too bad she lost that race."

Oh? Cali thought. That was curious. Karlyn had been bouncing with the other girls when Zack won.

"It would have been fun to see the disappointment on Stacy's face," she said.

Lunch was held in the half of the gym with the pullout tables. The sounds of two hundred children's voices echoed off the roof and rained back down like a waterfall, all jumbled and indecipherable. The aroma of mashed potatoes, gravy, rolls, and chicken nuggets filled the air. Cali looked at the food on her tray and wondered where to sit. She spotted Veronica and Rosalie sitting together, their backs to her. She was half tempted to go sit with them even though they were just fourth graders. Veronica suddenly turned around as if looking for her. Cali stepped behind two other kids to avoid being seen.

Karlyn solved her problem. "Cali," she called from halfway up the tables where she stood. She waved. "Let's go back here."

Had Karlyn been waiting for her? Once again she felt flattered.

Drop it, Dad, she said before he could begin. *She's just being pleasant.*

Still, he would have been right to speak. Whether or not Karlyn meant to flatter her, Cali felt flattered. She knew she wouldn't have felt the same way if someone from Bus 13 asked her to sit with them. That was because they didn't have ties to the pretty, popular girls at the school.

"I thought you'd be sitting with Stacy and Brittan," Cali said.

"I was," she said. "But all they can talk about is Zack and Lewis."

"I thought you liked them to talk about Zack and Lewis."

"I do, but not like them. They talk like they don't realize Zack and Lewis are still just stinky boys."

Cali laughed. Just the other day her Mom had been talking about the stinky boys who were in her sixth grade class. She had eventually married the stinkiest of them all.

That stink is what makes me a better lawyer than you, her dad said. He wasn't offended by lawyer jokes.

"Besides," Karlyn went on. "When I told them I thought Shelley had pretty eyes, they laughed at me."

Karlyn led Cali to a table at the end. They sat down among kids Cali didn't know. Before she could dig into the potatoes she recognized Zack. He was sitting at the end of the far row of tables across the gym amid a group of boys. Zack may be kind of cute, but he was still stinky, especially after those races this morning.

A small commotion beyond Zack got her attention. A boy was sitting with the rest, but he didn't have a lunch tray. He had playfully attempted to steal a roll from one of this friend's trays and gotten his hand slapped and arm punched for the trouble.

He wasn't deterred long. After a few moments of watching the other boys eat he quickly reached across the table and snatched another boy's chocolate milk. The boy grabbed his wrist before he escaped and, in the wrestling that ensued, the chocolate milk spilled. Several boys scooted back quickly to avoid the brown milk running off the table. A teacher called out and started walking their way. By the time the teacher got there the boys had applied their napkins to the mess and were pointing their fingers at the boy who had tried to steal the food.

"That's Jonathan," Karlyn said, following Cali's eyes. "He's always begging food off the other guys."

"Why doesn't he buy his own lunch?"

"I think he's behind on his lunch money. I saw the lunch lady turn him away the other day. She's pretty strict. She'll cut off anyone."

"You'd think his mom would at least send him with a lunch," Cali said.

"That'd be the day my mom made me a lunch," Karlyn said with a snort. Mashed potato fell onto her chin. She wiped it off with her hand and then licked her hand clean. "She's still in bed when I go to school."

Cali broke her roll in half and put some mashed potatoes and gravy on it before biting it.

"My dad eats his potatoes like that," Karlyn said, laughing.

Across the room Jonathan got up and walked away from the other boys. He reached the wall and turned to watch the other boys eat. He had messy brown hair and freckles. He looked just like the other stinky boys, but hungrier.

Cali spotted Felicia carrying her lunch tray down the aisle in Jonathan's direction. Her frizzy hair bounced as she walked and Cali could see the glint of her braces from all the way across the room.

Cali assumed Felicia was looking for a place to eat her lunch, but Felicia stopped next to Jonathan. Felicia said something before handing Jonathan her tray.

Oh, gee whiz, Felicia, Cali thought. *You gave me your breakfast and now you give Jonathan your lunch? There's such a thing as being too nice.* Cali was bothered that she hadn't thought of doing the same thing. *Of course, even if I thought of it, I wouldn't have done it,* she thought.

Felicia turned and started walking away as Jonathan stood looking confused. He studied the tray as if looking for a trick. Had she poured

146

salt on the potatoes or squeezed ketchup into the roll? Apparently satisfied that it was no joke he looked after Felicia.

One of the boys at the table, who had seen the whole thing, yelled something at Jonathan and laughed. Taking his lead the other boys joined in and made quite a sport of it. Jonathan blushed. With an angry expression he marched up the aisle. He pushed past Felicia and dumped the food, tray and all, into the trash. The boys were silent for half a second, stunned. They talked uncomfortably among themselves for a moment, then Zack laughed loudly and the others followed suit. Jonathan put his hands in his pockets and slunk out the door.

Cali didn't care about Jonathan at this point; it was Felicia she watched. Felicia stopped short when she saw what Jonathan did. Cali felt a pain knife through her heart. She felt it, but the pain wasn't her own.

Felicia.

"Ow," she said, bringing her hand to her chest. How could it be that someone as strong and kind as Felicia could feel so much pain?

"Look at this," Karlyn said, getting ready to squeeze mashed potatoes out of her mouth. She had missed the whole thing.

"I'll be right back," Cali said, jumping up. She ran along the line of tables, then turned up the aisle. Felicia had recovered her composure and was walking toward the door.

"Felicia." Cali sprinted up to her. "Come here. There's someone I want you to meet." She took Felicia's arm and turned her back down the aisle before she could decline. This was stupid. Surely Felicia already knew who Karlyn was. It was the only thing she could think of to keep Felicia from hurting alone.

"Ow," she said again, putting her hand over her chest.

"What?" Felicia said.

Cali thought she saw a look of concern on Felicia's face. *For me? When you're hurting so bad?*

"Nothing," Cali said as she led her up the row of tables.

As they passed the group of boys Cali pushed Felicia ahead and leaned down. "Pigs!" she said. For good measure she added, "Idiots!"

She was ashamed of herself even as the words came out of her mouth

Strong emotions make for weak arguments, said her mother. She had cried once in court and it hadn't gone well.

I wasn't trying to win an argument, Mom, she thought. *I was just expressing myself.* But she was still ashamed. She noticed the boys leaning back to see who that girl was. She was certain she was going to be sorry later. She caught Zack's eyes for a moment and wrinkled her nose at him.

"Karlyn, this is Felicia," Cali said when they reached her seat.

"I remember when you started school here a little while ago," Felicia said.

"Yeah. You invited me to play basketball that first recess."

"Sit," Cali said pushing Felicia down into what had been her own seat. "Scoot," she said to a couple of girls who were sitting right next to Felicia. They looked up, annoyed, but they scooted.

"I couldn't eat all this lunch," Cali said. "There's enough here for two, and we are going to share."

There are many people in the world who don't have the graciousness to accept someone else's attempt at kindness. Cali was fairly certain Felicia was not one of these. Besides, she had to be hungry by now.

"Look, we put the mashed potatoes on the rolls and we don't have to share a fork," Cali said.

Felicia flashed Cali a silvery grin.

Ow! Cali thought, flinching with the pain. She struggled to keep from bringing her hand to her chest. She smiled; the pain had been less this time.

"I love your hair," Karlyn said eyeing Felicia's frizzy mass.

Felicia and Cali stared at Karlyn to see if she was being sarcastic.

"No, really," she said.

She put her hands on either side of Felicia's head and squeezed the hair in towards Felicia's ears. Then she let go. The hair slowly poofed back out, each strand making its own space.

"That is so cool," Karlyn said with enthusiasm.

Felicia and Cali stared at Karlyn. It was difficult to believe what she had just done. Cali studied Felicia to see what she was going to do.

She brought her hand to her chest, not because of pain, but because she realized the pain was gone.

Felicia laughed. She laughed so loud that kids from the other tables turned and looked. "No one has ever done that before," she said.

Karlyn blushed. "That was wrong, wasn't it?" she said, as Felicia laughed again. "I've been wanting to do that since I first met you. I just did it without thinking. I'm sorry."

Felicia's laugh was so infectious that Cali laughed, too. Finally Karlyn joined in.

"I mean, your hair lives. My hair just lays there hibernating, or maybe it's totally dead."

Felicia and Cali stopped laughing and stared at Karlyn's hair. It cascaded in thick black waves off her head and over her shoulders. The absurdity of someone complaining about such beautiful hair hit Felicia and Cali at the same time. They burst into a new peal of laughter. Karlyn understood and joined them.

Karlyn stopped laughing first. Her smile was replaced by a mixture of curiosity and revulsion. She was looking past Felicia to the tables behind them.

Marty and Marcus sat at a table with a fancy glass water bottle in front of them. The water bottle was the kind with stylized etching on the sides and a rubberized screw-off lid. They had taken the lid off and were preparing to pour in some chocolate milk. That didn't explain the crowd that was starting to grow around them. Cali understood when she saw Marty grandiosely pour the milk from at least eighteen inches above the water bottle—he was putting on a show.

"Some ketchup if you please," said Marty.

One of the boys in the group handed him three packages of ketchup. Marcus opened each of them and squeezed the sticky, red contents into the water bottle.

"Gross," said a girl with thick glasses and pigtails who squeezed into a prime spot near Marcus.

"Not when you understand the chemical principles," Marcus said. "Now, for a key ingredient."

He pulled out a packet of soy sauce, the kind you get with Chinese takeout. He ripped it open and poured it in. It laid on the chocolate milk like grease on water, right next to floating globs of ketchup.

"Gross," said the girl, again.

"If you are going to keep saying that each time I put in an ingredient it's going to get very tedious," replied Marty.

"Gravy?" Marcus asked.

"Of course," answered Marty. "The soy sauce demands it."

Marcus spooned in some gravy. Some of it ran down the inside wall of the bottle. The girl was about to say 'gross' again. A warning glance from Marty stopped her.

"Now, I'll need a little of that cream soda, please," Marty said, to a kid on the far side of the group.

"This cream soda?" the boy asked.

"Robby Feldman, who else at Red Canyons Elementary drinks cream soda?" asked Marcus.

"Are you sick in any way or do you have any communicable diseases that I should know about?"

"What kinds of diseases?" asked Robby.

"I'll take that as a 'no,'" said Marty. He took the can of soda and poured a few ounces into the bottle. "That ought to do it," he said.

"What about a chicken nugget or two?" asked a heavy set boy enthusiastically. He stood four inches taller than any other boy in the room.

"Excuse me?" said Marty indignantly.

"This is not a fanciful witch's brew," Marcus added, "but a scientifically researched energy recipe that will turn anyone who drinks it—and keeps it down, I might add—into something similar to the Hulk."

"I'll drink it," said the big boy. "I love the Hulk."

Marty eyed the boy appraisingly and then said, "Very well, Max, but let me mix it first. Everyone, stand back."

A few of the kids actually moved back.

Cali knew that if they had seen what happened on the bus they would move much further back.

Marty screwed the lid on and shook the bottle vigorously. The goopy liquid splashed and coated the sides of the bottle with a brown-black glaze.

"It's okay, say it," Marcus said, nodding.

"Gross!" The girl blurted out the word as if it had been building up for a while.

"Come, prepare for the power," Marty said, signaling to Max.

"Awright," he said.

Marty unscrewed the lid and handed him the bottle. "Try to control yourself after you drink. We don't want you to hurt anyone."

"Y'all better watch out," Max said, and then took a gulp.

Cali saw him try to swallow. Then she saw him try to swallow again. Either the concoction was hanging onto his, or his throat had set up a roadblock to keep the gloop out. It was clear the drink was going to come out of his mouth the same way it went in.

Max's eyes grew big and started watering. He dropped the bottle which Marcus, being prepared, caught rather niftily. Max turned and ran for the garbage can.

"Notice his increased speed," Marty called out. "And he hasn't even swallowed yet."

Max didn't make it to the garbage can. He spewed the liquid all over the floor in front of him. Cheers, laughter, and groans rang through the gym. The teacher on lunch monitor duty came swiftly, but couldn't reach Max without stepping through the mess on the floor. Max looked innocently at the teacher and then pointed to Marty.

Marty, undeterred by the teacher's gaze, climbed up on a seat and called out, "Behold, the power!" and in two big gulps finished off the drink to even bigger cheers and groans.

The teacher pointed at Marty and opened his mouth to say something. Before he could, Marty yelled, "Just try and catch me before I get to the principal's office." He took off in a flash toward the back doors of the gym. The crowd cheered. The cheers grew louder as the teacher stumbled around the tables to chase him.

Karlyn's mouth hung open as she watched the spectacle. She turned and looked at Cali.

"Bus 13," Cali said, nodding.

"Hey" said an angry voice.

Cali turned to see Zack and three of his minions staring at her.

"Yeah, New Girl," Zack said when their eyes met.

"Human beings call me Cali," Cali said. She winced at her snarkiness. Being snarky was something new to her. Zack seemed to bring it out of her.

"Whatever," he said. His eyes were green under a semi-orderly mop of brown hair. His face didn't look as mean as his voice sounded. "Why did you say those things to us back there?" he said.

Cali knew very well the things he was referring to. The lawyer instincts she inherited from her parents told her that having him repeat them would be to her advantage. "What things?"

"Pi—" he began, but then he noticed how many kids had turned to watch the confrontation. Apparently he was smarter than he looked. He decided he didn't want everyone to know the exact words she had used to describe him. "Those rude things," he finished.

He was making this so easy. All she had to do was ask him, loudly, if 'pig' and 'idiot' were the rude things he was talking about. She would be up a point. The snarkiness she had felt moments earlier failed her now. It was true, her words had been rude. *No excuse can take the rudeness out of a rude person* her mother said.

The unsnarky Cali found herself at a disadvantage. If she let Zack get the next sentence in he would be in control of the conversation.

Her highly intelligent and graceful mother in a weak moment had actually asked her dad one day "Do these pants make me look fat?" Cali understood that all direct answers to this question are losers. Her dad, using his 'stinkiest boy lawyer intelligence' found a way out. He said he actually learned the technique from watching politicians. *You have to redirect* he said.

"Do you remember the first time I kissed you?" he asked his wife.

Cali watched her Mom melt as she remembered. She melted so much that Cali had to leave the room.

What can I redirect to? Cali thought desperately. *The topic of kissing isn't going to work here.*

She saw Shelley meandering the open end of the gym and had an inspiration.

"Did you know that Shelley *let* you beat her in the race this morning?" Cali asked.

Zack was silent as the wheels of his brain burned rubber making the turn onto the new road of thought.

"Wha—?" he said.

"It's true," Cali said casually. "Shelley is so much faster than you. She just doesn't like to embarrass people."

"That's stupid," Zack said, sputtering a little. "Everyone saw."

"Not everyone saw," Cali said, doubling down on her bluff. "They believe me that Shelley let you win."

She watched as expressions of disbelief, suspicion, and anger crossed his face.

"You could let them see again," Cali offered, lightly. Then, more seriously, she added, "Unless you're afraid you'll lose this time."

Zack hesitated. He had won by such a wide margin this morning that there was no debate. Yet here she was debating. For a moment she thought he was going to do the intelligent thing and refuse. His stinky-boy ego led him astray.

Winning points on his dramatic ability he slowly raised his arm and pointed at her. "Okay, at afternoon recess." Then he caught Cali by surprise. "But tomorrow at lunch, after I show everyone how wrong you are, you have to stand up on a seat and yell as loud as you can, 'I'm the stupid new girl.'"

Okay, she thought. *Now Zack is acting intelligently—kind of.*

She had manipulated him into running another race. He had every right to refuse, but if he didn't it was going to cost her. She would have been impressed at his strategy if what he was asking her to do wasn't so stupid.

Their little confrontation had gained a surprisingly large audience. So many eyes turned on her that she had a sudden rush of butterflies in her stomach. There was no way she could decline.

"Agreed," she said, trying to keep a squeak out of her voice.

With that the boys swiveled and left using extra swagger in their walk. Cali slowly sat down taking the weight off of her trembling legs, wondering how big a mistake she had just made.

CHAPTER 21 – LIKE THE WIND

Karlyn stared at Cali. When she found her voice she said, "You hide it pretty well at first, but you're a crazy girl, aren't you?"

Ignoring Karlyn Cali turned to Felicia. "You've seen how fast Shelley can run, right?" She needed confirmation that she wasn't crazy, as Karlyn put it.

"I heard she raced Zack this morning and lost," Felicia said.

"She didn't lose," Cali said, stubbornly. "She didn't try. Forget the race. Just tell me that you know how fast she is." If Felicia would just give her a wink or a nod she would feel so much better.

Cali had only known Shelley for a few hours and had seen wonders. Surely someone like Felicia, who had been riding the bus a long time, would have seen, too.

Felicia wanted to agree with Cali just to make her feel better. She began to nod, but her conscience won. At the last moment she shook her head. "I've never seen Shelley run," she said.

"Oh, no," Cali said, her heart sinking.

"*You* saw her run this morning." Felicia said.

"Of course I saw her run this—" Cali began. Was Felicia mocking her about having Shelley race again after her dismal loss? Then Cali realized that Felicia wasn't asking a question; she was reminding Cali of something—the incident with the wolves. Felicia hadn't seen what happened out in the fog, but she knew Cali had.

"Yes, I saw her run," Cali said, remembering.

154

"She was fast?"

"Like the wind."

"I wish I could have seen," Felicia said, closing her eyes.

Felicia's unquestioning faith gave Cali hope.

I could hug you, Cali thought, looking admiringly at Felicia.

Karlyn, on the other hand, had no faith. "I don't know what you two are talking about. I still want to know why you did that. Zack won't forget. He is going to win and make you stand up and tell everyone how stupid you are."

Cali opened her mouth to defend herself. What came out was, "I need to go talk to Shelley." To Felicia she said, "You, eat. I'm not hungry." Cali made her way to the side of the gym without lunch tables.

Shelley looked up and smiled when she saw Cali. "Hello," she said, putting her arm through Cali's. They strolled together like women of olden times did in long dresses through parks. Cali had never strolled arm in arm with anyone before.

Kids were running around the open part of the gym playing their games. None of them paid any attention to Cali and Shelley. As they walked across the gym Cali noticed Karlyn watching them. That didn't bother her. The looks and pointed fingers of Zack and his friends did. She blushed feeling ashamed. The blush was because they were making fun of her. The shame was because she was blushing.

Cali and her Dad watched shows like *To Kill a Mockingbird* and *Twelve Angry Men*. She was well-versed in his lectures on doing the right thing even when it isn't popular. Maybe walking arm-in-arm wasn't necessary, but pulling her arm free would not be the right thing to do. She took a deep breath and let it out slowly.

"Shelley?" she said.

Should she ask Shelley to race Zack again? Shelley came to a stop. Cali looked to see where Shelley was looking. Jimmy was on the stage. It wasn't much of a stage, just two steps up from the gym floor. It had black curtains hanging in the back and some colored lights aiming at it from racks on the ceiling. Jimmy stood at a microphone front, center stage. Behind him were worn-looking props from old productions, and instruments—an upright piano, a marimba, a set of drums, an electric guitar, and a tuba.

The tuba was the saddest looking instrument Cali had ever seen.

Its bell was bent on the side from being tipped over too many times.

Jimmy tapped on the microphone and then spoke. The microphone was on, but with bad acoustics, along with all the lunch time noise, she couldn't understand him. She did hear the word 'fugue,' though.

"What's he doing?" Cali asked.

"It's Open Mic Monday," Shelley said.

Open Mic Monday? Jimmy was going to perform something in front of this raucous crowd? Was Jimmy brave, or did a kid who wore plaid shorts and gym socks just not know enough to stay out of the public eye? Jimmy walked to the marimba and picked up the mallets. Looking at Cali he smiled. Cali glanced around self-consciously.

Jimmy took four mallets and positioned two in each hand holding the handles between his knuckles. Then he began to play. Cali looked around. Nobody in the gym was listening to him except her and Shelley. Cali, still arm-in-arm with Shelley, walked toward the stage to hear him better.

When she got close enough she recognized the music. He was playing Bach's *Toccata and Fugue in D Minor* again. Unlike on the bus with his pipe organ he didn't rattle any windows. The notes, in all their woodenness, bounced and danced their way through the opening run barely audible above the lunchroom din. Just before the final earth-shaking low note Jimmy sat the mallets down and skipped to the tuba. He got on his knees, and blew a mighty, gym-shaking note.

The kids noticed this. Jimmy stood, smiled broadly, and bowed. Some kids cheered, others jeered. Jimmy didn't appear to care. He looked at Cali and blew her a kiss with a mighty wave of his arm. He was so confident and cute that he was charming. Cali laughed and clapped.

"You know, I think that kid has talent," said a voice behind them. "That actually sounded like music."

Cali and Shelley turned to see the lunch room monitor standing there.

"Ya think," Shelley said with a hint of energy.

Cali was caught off guard. This was the Shelley she wanted to talk to. Cali took her arm and led her away from the teacher who looked like he was trying to find a reason to give them detention.

"Shelley, I'm wondering if you would do me a favor," she said.

The smile left Shelley's face.

Annnnd she's back to her spacey self, Cali thought. In spite of this Cali blurted out, "I was wondering if you would race Zack again. At afternoon recess?"

"Race Zack again?" Shelley said, slowly.

Cali grimaced at her words. *Well, I am the stupid new girl,* she thought.

"I don't know about racing," Shelley went on. "I just love to run."

Cali wanted to shake Shelley. *Do this for me! Where is the Shelley who took charge in the fog?* Looking into Shelley's depthless blue eyes Cali grew calmer. Shelley was looking at her like a small child would, with trust and even a little admiration. Cali realized that she had the power to talk Shelley into racing Zack. She could come up with an argument, most of it true, which would motivate Shelley to race. That would be manipulation.

Manipulation is a legitimate tool in the law, and in life, her father said.

But most often it's a dirty tool, her mother added.

Cali made a decision—she would just have to lose the bet with Zack. "I know you love to run. When I saw you leading those wolves over the ridge this morning I thought it was the most beautiful thing I had ever seen."

Shelley looked at Cali and glowed. "You saw me run?"

"How could I miss it? You were amazing. That's why I couldn't get Warren back to the bus. He wanted to run like you."

"You said 'beautiful,' Shelley said. "That's how I feel when I run. Beautiful and strong."

"That's only right," Cali said.

"I'll run with Zack," Shelley said, "if he wants to run."

"Oh, I don't know if he likes to run. I think he only likes to win races." Cali was sure of this. She had seen no joy in Zack until he crossed the finish line.

"I could show him what running is," Shelley said.

"I don't think he would care to watch you," Cali said, grumpily.

"At the race? Wouldn't he have to watch me in the race?"

Cali saw hope and excitement on Shelley's face. "If you were ahead of him he couldn't help but watch you," she said.

Is this really happening? Cali wondered. *She's going to race, er, run? And I'm not manipulating her, Mom,* she added.

"Then let's run at recess," Shelley said.

Cali saw Shelley's eyes glow just for an instant.

Before lunch was over word of the race spread throughout the school. Even Mrs. Earl heard.

"I hear you like to race," Mrs. Earl said, stopping by Cali's desk.

"No, not me," Cali said, feeling the eyes of her classmates turning her direction. "It's Shelley who runs."

"Shelley Narf?" Mrs. Earl asked, unable to hide her surprise.

Cali had hoped that Mrs. Earl would be one who could see more in Shelley than just a wounded girl.

Cali looked down and nodded. She didn't want to discuss it with nonbelievers.

"I ran when I was younger," said Mrs. Earl.

Cali glanced up, surprised to see Mrs. Earl still standing there.

"I think I would have run a marathon if they had allowed women to run then. Well, more power to her," she said.

It had been one of the warmest Januarys Warburton had ever seen. At afternoon recess kids, most without coats, crowded the edge of the field. The sight of all the kids sent the butterflies in Cali's belly into a tizzy of fluttering. Karlyn had made a point of walking out with Cali even though Cali hadn't asked her to.

What have I gotten myself into? she wondered. Seven years at East Heights Elementary and most of the kids there wouldn't realize she was gone. One day at Red Canyon Elementary and she was in the middle of everything.

Devon came trotting by. He gave her a thumbs up and a smile as he passed. His raccoon tail whapped one shoulder, then the other as he ran.

"It's Bus 13," she mumbled. She would have slipped into Red

Canyon Elementary as quiet as a mouse if it hadn't been for Bus 13.

"What?" asked Karlyn.

"Nothing."

Would Shelley even show up? She might forget. Maybe a teacher would keep her in, or maybe she had another appointment with the counselor.

". . . and if she loses the new girl has to dance naked on the table at lunch tomorrow," said a passing boy.

"No way. The teachers wouldn't allow it," responded his friend.

"She has to," said the first boy.

"Idiots," said Karlyn.

Oh, I wish I would have eaten something at lunch, she thought, putting her hand on her stomach. *Or maybe that would just make it worse.*

One of Zack's minions saw Cali and the cry went out, "Here she comes." The crowd parted and she saw Zack at the starting line. He looked ready to go.

"So, where is she?" he said. He sounded extra tough when he spoke, but Cali was sure she heard nerves under it all.

"I don't know. It's not like I own her or anything. She doesn't even have to show up if she doesn't want to." The words tumbled uncontrolled out of Cali's mouth.

"If she doesn't show you forfeit and have to pay up," Zack said.

"She's going to have to dance on the—" started a boy

"Shut up," yelled Karlyn.

Zack's as nervous as I am, Cali thought. *I wonder why.*

In answer to her unspoken question she heard Brac's voice in her ear.

"I told him some stories about Shelley. That shook him up a little."

Cali turned to see Brac and his happy-go-lucky grin. He actually looked handsome.

"You know how fast Shelley is?" she asked.

"Nope. Never seen her run. Just made some things up to psyche Zack out."

Cali's heart struggled between disappointment and a desire to hug

Brac. He slipped away into the crowd.

"There she is," someone yelled.

The crowd parted. Shelley walked—no—meandered toward the group. The kids quieted as they watched her come. Everyone wondered how Shelley could be expected to race Zack. Cali knew Shelley was fast, but she had no idea what would happen when the race began.

There was whispering among the kids. Shelley had taken off the jeans she was wearing under her dress. Her sneakers were untied. It was a balmy 55 degrees with sunshine, but Shelley looked woefully underdressed for a January.

"I could make her win," said a pugnacious little voice.

Cali jumped. Rosalie was standing at her elbow.

Cali should have dismissed that idea immediately. The sight of underdressed, meandering Shelley worried her so much that she hesitated.

"You really could, couldn't you?" Cali said.

"You bet," Rosalie said.

Thoughts danced through Cali's brain. With Rosalie's help Shelley would win for sure. Shelley might win without help, but the possibility she might lose because she didn't care about winning was killing Cali.

No one would know, and the results would be just as they should be, Cali thought.

A vibration in the air and a faint buzzing sound in her ears brought Cali out of her thoughts. She looked down at Rosalie. Her face showed intense concentration and her eyes had a faraway look. Rosalie was moving ahead with her suggestion. What would she do, break Zack's leg? Give Shelley wings? Her curiosity almost got the best of her. She remembered Rosalie saying something about 'forcing people' and 'bad magic.' To have Shelley win against her will—there was something of 'bad magic' about that.

"Rosalie, stop!" she said.

Rosalie showed no sign of stopping

Cali dropped to a knee facing Rosalie and grabbed her by the arms. "No, Rosalie. Stop it!" She shook her.

The buzzing stopped. Rosalie's eyes slowly focused on Cali.

"I thought—" Rosalie stuttered. "I—" She was acting dazed. Cali was looking for signs that Rosalie was going to faint. Had she gone that far? When a tear appeared in her eye, Cali knew she was going to be all right.

Bringing her face closer to Rosalie she whispered, "She needs to do this by herself."

Shelley finally arrived. She smiled at Cali and then looked at Zack. "Shall we run?" she said. She said it lightly, politely, as if she were asking him to dance.

Zack studied Shelley as if he were trying to understand what she meant, as if this was a trick. "Whatever you want to call it," he said, "but let's go."

Zack got in his starting crouch. Shelley slipped her shoes off and stepped beside him.

"What are you doing?" Zack said. "You can't run barefoot."

"I like to feel the Earth when I run," she said in that spacey way of hers.

"Whatever, but you can't blame losing on running barefoot."

Shelley didn't reply.

From behind Cali heard, "I don't care what they say, she is freaky."

Cali whirled to find herself facing Stacy and Brittan. Cali struggled to hold back angry words. She felt a vibration in the air and looked down to see Rosalie focusing hard on the two girls. She nudged Rosalie with the back of her hand. Rosalie looked up at her, annoyed. The vibration stopped.

"I think 'peculiar' is what you really mean," Cali said.

Stacy and Brittan, startled, nodded.

"Ready."

Cali whirled back to face the starting line.

"Set." It was one of Zack's minions.

"Go!"

Zack exploded off the starting line. Once again Zack was so anxious for speed that his body got a little ahead of his feet and he stumbled. Managing not to fall, he corrected and was off.

Shelley just stood and watched. In that instant, as much as Cali dreaded Zack crossing the finish line, she realized it was okay. There was something pure and beautiful about whatever it was that separated Shelley from the petty drama around her.

At the moment Zack recovered from his stumble, Shelley turned her head and smiled at Cali. Cali saw the light in her eyes. Shelley was the wind and the clouds and the wolves running over the ridge. And then she was off.

Shelley ran so lightly that she appeared to float, like when a deer leaps over a fence. Her legs flashed in the sun. Her dress fluttered behind her. She gained on Zack so quickly that Cali looked down at Rosalie.

"It's not me," Rosalie said, watching Shelley in awe.

Shelley passed Zack and crossed the finish line two steps ahead of him.

CHAPTER 22 – BAD MAGIC

As Zack stumbled to a stop, gasping for breath, Shelley kept on running. She sailed over the grass as smoothly as a balloon on the wind. Her legs were a blur. She never slowed. The kids stood with their mouths open, watching in wonder.

"You knew she could run like this? Rosalie asked, in a low voice.

Cali had forgotten to breathe as she watched. She drew in a deep breath and nodded.

"Wow," Rosalie said, summing up her feelings.

Shelley reached the end of the field and turned to follow the chain-link fence to the far side. At the far side she turned with the fence and began crossing back in front of the kids. The sun lit up her yellow dress and she glowed like a golden comet.

Cali felt a breeze on her face and smelled pine trees. And then, as if from miles away, she heard the high, piercing pitch of a howling wolf. On the other side of the fence was an empty lot that rose up a small hill. On top Cali saw fog swirling in the sunlight. A wolf in the fog was watching Shelley run. It was Sheila.

"Um, Cali?" Rosalie asked, sounding troubled. "Do you see the wolf?"

"Yes," Cali said, relieved that Rosalie saw it, too. It was one thing to see the wolves while on Bus 13, but it was totally unexpected at recess.

"Good," said Rosalie. "For a moment I thought that using my magic so much in one day broke my mind."

Cali became aware of Karlyn staring at her. "What?" she said, looking from Cali to Rosalie.

Oh, great, thought Cali. *Karlyn and her big ears.*

Cali thought fast. "Inside joke," she said. "A Bus 13 thing."

"Joke?" she asked. "But I thought I heard a . . . well, something, too."

Rosalie and Cali were startled. Had Karlyn heard the wolf? Not sure what to do, they glanced at each other then shrugged.

A wailing sound erupted behind Cali. It was similar to the wolf, but sadder. She turned to see Stacy standing there in tears.

"Don't you dare laugh at me," Stacy blubbered fiercely. "I don't know what's wrong with me. I watch her run and I cry."

Stacy's tears were infectious. They made Cali want to cry.

"No, it's okay," Cali said. "She's just so beautiful when she runs."

"But it's not her makeup or her hair or her clothes; it's something else, isn't it?" Stacy said. She was struggling to understand this kind of beauty. Her nose was running.

"Yes, it's something deeper," Cali said, turning back to watch Shelley. She was running down the fence line toward them, now.

"Do you think she could teach me to run like that?" Stacy asked.

Cali hesitated. "Um, I don't think it can be taught."

"Well," Stacy said, swallowing disappointment, "do you think at least she would let me be her friend?"

Stacy's question sent a pain through Cali's heart so sharp it almost took her breath away. If she knew anything about Shelley it was that she would be anyone's friend, even Stacy.

What is wrong with me? she thought, struggling to answer Stacy's question. *Jealousy?* She had never been jealous in her life.

Jealousy is a potential side-effect of caring, her father said.

That's why I don't do the friend thing, she had told her father.

You like living life as a rock? he asked.

"Stacy?" Brittan said, sounding a little jealous herself.

"Brittan, beauty is more than a pretty face and lustrous hair," Stacy said, clearly having an epiphany.

That's what I always say, said Cali's Mom.

Nobody asked you, Cali thought, *but you're right, as usual.*

"When I watch Shelley run I understand," Stacy said. "Maybe she'll let you be her friend, too, Brittan." Stacy looked at Cali for confirmation.

"Of course she would," Cali said, trying to swallow the bitter taste jealousy left in the back of her throat.

"But if you do anything to hurt her—," Rosalie said, looking at Stacy, eyes narrowed.

Cali stopped her from saying more with a nudge of her arm.

Shelley, looking like she could go around again, came to a gentle stop at the starting line. She breathed deeply, but there was no gasping or pain on her face. Nobody clapped or said anything. They just gathered around her in respectful silence and stared like they were trying to figure out what she was. She looked over at Cali and beamed with joy. Cali, finding no words, just smiled and nodded.

The crowd suddenly parted as Zack pushed his way through.

Uh oh, thought Cali. *Time for the dramatics.*

Zack only looked at Shelley with the same look of amazement as everyone else. He turned to one of his minions and said, "Did you see that?"

His minion nodded.

"That was amazing," he said, looking Shelley in the eyes. Then he looked at her feet. "I ought to try running barefoot.".

Everyone laughed. The crowd started breaking up. Stacy pushed past Cali and Rosalie on her way to talk with Shelley.

"Ah, now we don't get to see the new girl dance nak—"

"Shut up, Bruce," Karlyn said. She went over and stomped on his foot. An argument began.

Cali and Rosalie stood wondering what to do now.

"What do you know about that wolf?" Rosalie asked, suspiciously.

"I only met her this morning," Cali said, looking for the wolf. Sheila was gone.

"Her?" Rosalie said. "Well, I don't like the way she looked at me right before she disappeared."

"She didn't look at you," Cali said. How could she tell from that distance?

"She *looked* at me," said Rosalie, determinedly.

Cali remembered how Sheila had turned to look at her from the top of the ridge. "Okay, but she won't hurt you." She said. More softly she added, "At least I don't think she would."

"When you see her again," Rosalie said, "You tell her she better not try to hurt me or anyone on that bus or I'll turn her into a kitten."

The image of a little kitten running across the mountain meadow made Cali laugh. Something in Rosalie's voice made her think twice. "Could you really do that?" asked Cali.

"Yes." There was no question about it.

Cali hesitated. "Have you ever done that to anyone . . . er, anything before?

Rosalie lowered her head and spoke quietly. "No."

"Then how do you know you can?"

"Oh, I know," she said softly. She looked down and went on. "I can feel it in there pushing to come out. It almost drives me crazy sometimes."

They walked slowly, aimlessly, around the playground. Cali could feel the energy radiating from Rosalie. If she didn't know better she would just pass it off as attention deficit disorder. It seemed like a quarter of the kids in school were diagnosed with that. There was far more than A.D.D. to Rosalie.

Glancing down she caught Rosalie in an unguarded moment. There was weariness on her face. It was no wonder with the secret she carried.

"Why *haven't* you ever done anything like that?" Cali asked.

"Bad magic," Rosalie said.

"Bad magic? Who told you that?"

"Nobody. I just know." She looked up at Cali with her serious eyes. "Using magic costs, and that kind of magic costs too much."

"Is that why you pass out when you use magic?"

Rosalie nodded. "And that's just when I light a candle or do something else harmless like that. Think what would happen if I tried to change people somehow."

The thought gave Cali the shivers.

"Cali?"

"Yes?" Their eyes met for a moment.

"I lied. I did try to do something once." Rosalie was silent for a moment. "My dad drinks. Once I used magic to stop him."

She quit talking and looked out at the kids on the field. Cali waited.

"I woke up in the hospital. They blamed my dad because he was drunk when he brought me there, but it wasn't him. It was the magic."

"Oh," Cali said, at a loss for words.

"So that's why I promised Mr. Fennelmyer not to do any magic at all," she said, looking suddenly cheery. "It's bad for me."

You must be having a really bad day, Cali thought.

"I've had a bad day," Rosalie said, apparently thinking the same thing. "But with you here, now, I'll do so much better." She looked up at Cali, a bright smile forming on her little mouth.

Cali wasn't sure she liked the sound of that. What did she have to do with Rosalie's magic? The thing about Bus 13 was they seemed to expect something from her. She didn't know what. She had heard her mom and dad talking about lawsuits that involved 'implied responsibility.' Bus 13 seemed to be forcing her to become involved. There was the prank with Freddy and Bric in class this morning. There was Veronica and Shelley. Being responsible for Rosalie was like bringing a tiger to school on a dog leash.

They wandered past some boys playing basketball. Arnold and Miguel were among them. Cali stopped to watch. They played basketball more like it was football. Sometimes they dribbled the ball, but often they carried it and tried to push their way to the basket. Arnold looked like he was in Heaven. Miguel, as usual, was getting the worst of it, but he was still smiling.

"That's Wes," Rosalie said, pointing to another big boy. "He's mean.

Meaner than Arnold? As she watched she could see what Rosalie meant. Arnold plowed through people and bounced other boys around with his weight advantage, but he did it with a happy smile, never intending harm. Wes took pleasure when others got hurt.

"He makes me so mad," Rosalie said, watching as he knocked Miguel down.

"He's okay," Cali said, watching Miguel get up. She was worrying more about Rosalie's temper than about Miguel's health.

You see, there's the implied responsibility. Cali didn't like it.

Wes, with the ball under his arm, tried to run through Arnold on the way to the basket. Arnold stiff-armed him and sent him to the ground on his side.

"Ha ha," Arnold said. "You'll think twice about doing that again, isn't that right, Miguel?"

Miguel trotted over and leaped to slap Arnold's high five. Even on the basketball court they were still a wrestling tag team.

Arnold looked over at Cali and Rosalie. "When they work, they work well, right?" He flexed his arms.

Rosalie blushed and laughed.

Cali was watching Wes. A look of pure hatred formed on his face. He looked past Arnold to the playground monitor who was strolling by looking the other way. Cali saw the plan form in Wes's mind, but not soon enough to do anything about it. Wes got up, and with a running start, shoved Miguel to the ground. Miguel hit the asphalt and slid on his chin. When he looked up there was blood.

Arnold stood, stunned, then turned in fury on Wes. Wes screamed. Yelling to get Mr. Menset's attention was part of his plan. Cali didn't think that he meant to scream like a girl.

"Mr. Menset!" he yelled, backing quickly away from Arnold.

Mr. Menset strode over.

"Arnold's playing too rough. He shoved Miguel down and when I tried to stop him he tried to hit me." He hid behind Mr. Menset.

Miguel, with blood dripping off his badly scraped chin, was a compelling sight. "Arnold, to the principal's office," he snapped as he helped Miguel up.

Cali was about to jump in for Arnold's defense, but she felt a vibration in the air and heard a buzzing sound. She looked down to see Rosalie completely focused on Wes. Cali knew that if Rosalie was half as angry at Wes as she was what was coming would be 'bad magic.'

"Rosalie, no," she said, grabbing her arm.

The buzzing got louder.

Cali knelt in front of Rosalie and looked into her eyes. Putting a hand on each shoulder she said, "Remember your promise."

Rosalie looked straight through Cali, her eyes still locked on Wes, but the buzzing faltered and weakened.

"Help," Rosalie said, in a small voice as if calling from another room.

Redirect, her mother said.

"Put his shoes on the wrong feet," Cali whispered. That seemed harmless enough.

Cali was embarrassed to suggest such a stupid trick. It paled in comparison to the toad or whatever she was going to turn Wes into. Rosalie smiled almost imperceptibly. A second later her eyes rolled back and she fell unconscious into Cali's arms.

Chapter 23 – Do I Care?

Mr. Menset was walking Miguel off the playground when he remembered that the principal would want to talk to Wes, also. He turned and said, "Wes, you come, too."

Wes took one step and fell flat on his face. When he looked up his nose was bleeding.

Mr. Menset's eyebrows shot up. "What the heck, Wes. Why would you do that?"

Wes, in complete confusion, tried to get up. He struggled, but couldn't get his legs to work right. He turned over and stared at his feet.

"How'd your shoes get tied together?" Mr. Menset asked standing over Wes. He looked again. "And you've got them on the wrong feet."

"I didn't do this," Wes sputtered. He looked scared. "Somebody . . . somebody . . ." he looked around desperately for this 'somebody.' His eyes fell on Arnold. Arnold, barely hiding his amusement, looked at him and shrugged.

"Somebody snuck up, switched your shoes, and tied the laces together while you were playing basketball and you didn't notice?" asked Mr. Menset. He sounded skeptical as well as confused.

"Yes! Somebody . . ." Wes went on still looking for an answer. His eyes found Cali and narrowed. Cali, still holding the unconscious Rosalie in both arms, looked back boldly. *If it wasn't for me you'd be a toad.*

"Never mind," Mr. Menset said struggling with the knot in Wes's shoelaces. "Just take them off. And hold your shirt to your nose until we get you to the office."

As he pulled Wes to his feet, Mr. Menset noticed Cali holding Rosalie. Rosalie's head rested on her shoulder with her face towards her neck. "Now what's wrong with her?" he asked, wondering how many things could go wrong in the space of one minute.

"She doesn't like the sight of blood," Cali said. "She'll be fine as soon as they leave."

Mr. Menset sighed and said, "You bring her in to the office if she doesn't feel better right away." He headed to the school with the three boys. Arnold, walking slightly behind Mr. Menset, looked back and smiled. He flexed his arms and pointed at Rosalie, then gave a thumbs up. Cali wasn't sure what he was trying to say exactly, but he was clearly sending happiness and approval their way. Wes, looking over his shoulder, saw Arnold's gesticulations. His eyes showed a mix of confusion, suspicion, and fear.

"Rosalie, wake up," Cali sang nervously. Some of the ball players were looking at them. She put her arms around Rosalie's waist and picked her up with a grunt. Rosalie was heavier than she looked. Cali spun around as if she were playing a game with Rosalie and angled off toward the grass. The boys lost interest.

She laid Rosalie on her back in the grass and wondered what to do next. If Rosalie got taken to the office like this she didn't know what would happen, but it wouldn't be good.

A shadow fell over her. Brac was looking down at them.

"Well, for the new girl you seem to be in the middle of everything interesting that goes on at Red Canyons," he said.

"Oh, be quiet and say something helpful," she said. "What do we do?"

"How should I know," Brac said. "She's only done magic here once before."

"What happened?"

"She made Barker's pants fall down."

Cali was tempted to ask more about this, but let it go. "No, not what did *she* do. What did *you* do after she did the magic?" Cali gave Brac an exasperated look.

"Gee whiz. Take it easy. What did I do? Nothing. She passed out as usual. When she wouldn't wake up they took her to the hospital. They did a bunch of tests. She didn't come back to school for two days."

"Oh great," said Cali. "If that happens again it could cause all kinds of complications. They might never let her come back to school."

"True," Brac said, nodding. He offered no suggestions.

"Rosalie, please wake up," Cali said, shaking her gently.

"Only time will wake her up," Brac said. "That's a well-documented fact."

"We don't have time," Cali said. *And why do I seem to care more than Brac does?* He stood with his hands in his pockets like they were discussing the weather.

Another shadow fell across Rosalie.

"Did you see Shelley run?" Marissa said. "She was incredible." She punched the air a couple of times in her excitement. Her raccoon tail bounced with each motion.

"Incredible?" said Brac. "Yes, I think you have chosen the best word for once."

"You're darn toot'in," Marissa said.

"Excuse me," Cali interrupted. "In case you haven't noticed, we have a problem here."

"We?" asked Brac.

Shocked, Cali looked up at him. "Don't you even care about Rosalie?"

Brac looked uneasy and didn't answer. Marissa glanced at Brac and then spoke. "It's not that," she said. "It's just that we're surprised you care."

Cali looked at them, hurt and disbelieving. "Why would you think I don't care?"

"You said things—" Marissa started.

"On the bus," Brac finished.

Freddy and Bric walked up.

"What? She did magic again?" Freddy asked.

"Clearly she's had a relapse," added Bric.

"I think Cali's a bad influence on her," said Marissa.

"Me? A bad influence?" Cali was so mad she sputtered.

"It's just that Rosalie hasn't done so much magic in one day since—" she thought for a moment, "well, since I've known her. Then you get on the bus and—"

"How dare you." Tears came to Cali's eyes. Letting them run down her face, she went on. "None of what's happened today has anything to do with me. My getting on Bus 13 was a mistake. Even Mr. Fennelmyer thinks so. I never asked to be Rosalie's friend. She just grabbed on to me and won't let go."

Cali took a moment to wipe her tears, and then her nose, on the back of her sleeve. "And let me tell you about my influence." She looked at the unconscious Rosalie. "The fact that Wes is still human is my influence. If I hadn't been there Wes would be a toad or something worse."

"So what did Rosalie do?" asked Marissa.

"Apparently she put his shoes on the wrong feet," said Brac. Then looking at Cali he added, "And tied his shoelaces together?"

"I didn't tell her to tie his shoelaces together," Cali said. "I only mentioned the shoes. She came up with the shoelaces on her own."

"That is *so* Rosalie," said Bric.

Everyone laughed. The laughter ebbed into an awkward silence. That's when Felicia and Shelley arrived. Felicia smiled her silvery smile when Cali looked up. Cali saw that Shelley's feet were still bare. *They must be so cold*, she thought. Between Shelley's legs Cali saw Jimmy jogging over in his clumsy way.

What is this, an impromptu Bus 13 reunion?

As if on cue Devon and Warren appeared as silently as woodsmen. The circle grew larger. Cali, on her knees next to Rosalie, was well-hidden from view.

Finally Brac spoke. "So, Cali, in spite of what you said on the bus, with everything that's happened today, you're telling us that you really do care about us?"

Cali hesitated.

Caring is the sweetest curse a person can ever suffer, her father said. *I can't remember who, but somebody important said that.*

Do I care? The possibility struck her dumb for a moment.

It occurred to Cali that being on her knees next to the unconscious Rosalie was evidence that maybe she did. It made her angry that the other kids who knew Rosalie better than she did were just standing around staring.

It's time to see how much they care.

Cali got up, brushed her knees off, and then pushed her way out of the circle.

One of them can take care of this mess.

Cali took five determined steps toward the school, weakened, and looked back. The kids were just standing there watching her, curiously. The space between Freddy and Bric where she had pushed through was still open. She could see Rosalie's little body where she had left it, lying motionless on the ground.

"What is wrong with you people?" she said loudly enough to catch the attention of some nearby kids. She glared at them and then marched back to Rosalie's side. "Maybe I do care. That doesn't mean I'm going to leave Rosalie here to be stared at by a bunch of kids who should know enough to help."

That didn't make any sense at all, her dad said.

I know, Dad, but a girl doesn't have to make sense to say something important.

Atta girl.

The bell rang. Kids started heading for the school doors like water running to a drain. Recess was over.

"What are you going to do?" asked Jimmy.

"I don't know. I guess just stay here with her until a teacher comes to yell at us, and then see what happens," Cali said in resignation.

"Excuse us," two voices said.

Devon and Warren stepped aside to let Marty and Marcus into the circle.

"How come nobody told us we were having a bus meeting?" Marcus said.

Marty nudged him in the ribs and pointed at Rosalie.

"Oh, dear," Marcus said. His eyebrows angled together as he thought. "Have you noticed that Rosalie uses magic more when Cali is—"

"Shut it," Brac said.

"We've already been there," noted Marissa. More softly she added, sincerely, "And I'm sorry."

Cali realized Marissa was talking to her.

"You guys go on in. No need for all of you to get in trouble. We'll be okay."

"Uh oh, Mrs. Williams is looking this way," said Jimmy glancing over his shoulder.

The kids moved restlessly, but no one left the circle. Devon pushed his hands deep into his pockets. He pulled something out and stared at it curiously. It was one of the vials that held the formula that woke Rosalie on the bus.

"Do you think this might still work?" he asked.

Marty and Marcus stared at the vial, and then at each other.

"How quickly did you put the stopper back on?" asked Marty.

"Real fast," Devon said. "Last time you made something like this on the bus it gave us all a headache."

"Perhaps there is enough residual chemical in the vial to—" started Marcus.

"Oh, just try it already," interrupted Freddy.

"Yes, do," added Felicia more calmly.

Cali held out her hand for the vial. Devon willingly gave it to her. He remembered how Rosalie woke up on the bus.

"Hey, you kids," called Mrs. Williams. "Didn't you hear the bell? Recess is over."

"Here she comes," said Veronica in a sing-song voice.

Cali put the vial close to Rosalie's nose and pulled the stopper. The vial looked empty. A second as long as eternity passed and nothing happened. Rosalie's eyes popped open and everyone in the circle stepped back. Rosalie sat up like a jack-in-the-box. She did not look happy. Her expression was frightening. Cali held her ground.

"I didn't tell you to tie his shoelaces together," Cali said "But it was a nice touch."

The icy look on Rosalie's face melted into a smile. She threw her arms around Cali's neck. "You stayed with me," she whispered.

I stayed with you, Cali repeated to herself.

"Hurry and get up," Marissa said softly in her sing-song warning voice, "She's almost here."

Felicia turned to Jimmy. "Isn't Mrs. Williams your teacher?" she asked.

"I got this," Jimmy said. Standing straight, he pulled his shorts up to his belly button. He turned to face the stout Mrs. Williams.

"Mrs. Williams, I noticed that you have prepared a new section in World History on the Pharaohs of Egypt. I can't tell you how disappointed I am that you didn't take my suggestion about the great composers of the world, primarily, Bach."

Caught off guard, Mrs. Williams focused on Jimmy, who positioned himself directly in front of her.

"Jimmy, you don't understand what the school requires of us teachers," she said. She looked past Jimmy to the other children. "Why aren't you kids going to class? Is detention that appealing to all of you?"

"Actually, detention is good study time," said Bric, thoughtfully.

"Yes, not a lot of distractions there," added Freddy.

"But the truth is," chimed in Felicia, "we were looking for Shelley's shoes."

Mrs. Williams looked down at Shelley's feet. "Good heavens, Shelley. You're barefoot in January?"

"That's how she runs," said Marissa. "You did see the race, didn't you?"

"Actually, I did," said Mrs. Williams. "Shelley, you do run beautifully. I don't know that I've ever seen anything like it." She thought for a moment and then added, "You won't believe it, but I ran the 880 when I was in high school."

"We do believe it," said Felicia not giving Mrs. Williams's stout size a second thought.

"You'd be surprised what we can believe," added Veronica, coyly.

The peculiar kids of Bus 13 surrounded Mrs. Williams as they walked across the empty playground toward the school doors. Mrs. Williams was telling a story of when she came from behind to almost win a big race. Cali and Rosalie followed the others. Rosalie reached up and took Cali's hand.

They were all late getting back to their classrooms. Mrs. Williams was so charmed by their interest in her athletic exploits that she spoke to each of their teachers for them. Finally, she remembered she had her own class to worry about. She and Jimmy rushed down the hall together.

The school buzzed with news of the race. It was the topic behind whatever subjects the teachers were finishing the day with.

Because of the race, Shelley's reputation jumped six levels in stature. Kids were talking.

"She beat Zack running barefoot."

"She's probably the fastest sixth grader in the state. I heard the high school coach is watching her."

"She's so quiet, but they're the ones who surprise you."

"That's how she got away from the people who took her. When she got the chance she ran and they couldn't catch her."

This new respect splashed over on Cali by association. Kids gave her sideways glances, the good kind. They were wondering if they had a chance at being her friend. During Mrs. Earl's impromptu lecture on great women in history she slipped Cali a wink.

Karlyn stayed close to Cali. She told the story of Cali's challenge to Zack three times. Cali was bolder and braver with each telling. When class was out for the day Cali had a loose group of kids hovering nearby. They were her entourage as she walked to the bus loading zone.

It was one of the most dangerous moments of my life, said her dad talking about the time he worked on a high profile case. There were lights and cameras and reporters yelling for his attention. He had to silence his phone due to all the calls for interviews. *It almost made me believe I was more important and smarter than I really was.*

I'd be silly to let it get to me, Dad, she thought. *That's what all this is, silliness, right?*

She had only set up a race that another girl had run and won.

It's not like I actually did anything.

But she had done something. She couldn't ignore that. She had stood up to the school jock.

Where did the courage for that come from?

The memory gave her tingles.

She had helped save Rosalie from the consequences of her magic. She still felt the warm fuzzies from that. There was that incident with Veronica. If she hadn't taken the time to help Veronica her father might have ended up in jail. Cali had made a difference. The tingles grew stronger. And—this one made her smile—she had uncovered the prank with Bric and Freddy. It had been a day like no other in her life.

Who are you? Mr. Fennelmyer's voice echoed in her head.

I'm still not sure, but it turns out I'm a lot more than I knew I was this morning, Cali thought.

Chapter 24 – Not Particularly Peculiar

Four buses lined up along the curb in the bus lane. Bus 13 was at the back of the line. Amid the crowd of pushing kids Cali saw raccoon tails zig-zagging their way along.

Karlyn was at Cali's side chatting away as they walked. She was telling Dianne, a little blond, blue-eyed fifth grader, about Cali's challenge to Zack. It was the fourth time Cali had heard it. She wasn't tired of it, yet.

"She looked him in the eye and said, 'So, you're afraid to race her again? That makes you a coward!'"

"She really said that to Zack?" asked Dianne, with wide eyes.

"I was there, wasn't I?" Karlyn asked, importantly.

Cali rolled her eyes and shook her head, but she didn't correct Karlyn. They reached the third bus in the line, Bus 31. The crowd of kids ended here. Bus 13 looked lonely in the back. She saw Mr. Fennelmyer through the big windshield. She looked away before they made eye contact.

Why did I look away?

She cringed at the question.

I don't have to answer that.

No, you don't, because you already know the answer, and it's not pretty.

Oh, be quiet!

A hand grabbing hers interrupted her argument. "Ride with us," Karlyn said, tugging her toward the door of Bus 31.

Stacy and Brittan stuck their heads out a back window and waved. "Come on, we have seats saved back here."

"Heads in the bus. And shut the window!" The harried-looking driver held the microphone up to her mouth and stared in the mirror.

Kids bumped Cali as they got on the bus. Cali hesitated. She glanced back. Bric and Brac were getting on Bus 13. Brac looked her way and waved. Her heart felt lighter—she didn't know why. She started to raise a hand to wave back when Freddy trotted up to Brac. Cali realized Brac had been waving to him, not to her. She felt a little sting in her heart.

Silly hurt, Cali thought. It didn't make her feel any better.

'Silly hurts' are those meaningless little things that ruin your day even though they aren't worthy of a second thought, said her mom.

Karlyn was saying, "The Kays used to live in your house and this bus stopped there every day until they moved."

Sitting in the back of the bus with popular girls? It was flattery. She knew it. She waited for her father's voice. Strangely, it didn't come. The silly hurt was in the way.

Why resist? What's one afternoon of self-indulgence?

"Okay," she said.

That simple word felt momentous. She felt as if she were doing something life-changing. The feeling was enhanced by the sense that she was being naughty. She could almost see the surprised looks of all those who knew her well. She relished it.

Karlyn, still holding her hand, led her up the steps.

"She lives where the Kays used to," Karlyn said to the bus driver.

"What's another rider in this crowd?" said the tired driver.

Cali followed Karlyn and Dianne up the narrow aisle pushing through knees and past seats of boisterous kids. This bus was full. One group of boys—they looked like second graders—were trading insults with another group.

"You're so stupid you stink."

"Yeah? Well, you're so stupid you don't even know you're stupid."

A paper airplane zipped by and hit a girl in the back of the head. The girl scooted up on her knees and looked for the culprit.

"Knock it off, Dan," the bus driver called over the intercom. "Turn around and sit down, Becca."

"Come on, you owe me," said a boy reaching his hand across the aisle. His hair was gelled into a pointy ridge down the middle of his head.

"No," the boy across the aisle replied, as he pulled the wrapper off his sucker and threw it on the floor. The boy with the hair said a word that made Cali blush.

When they reached the back Stacy looked at Dianne and said, "There's not room for you. Go sit with the fifth graders."

Dianne shrugged and squeezed past Karlyn and Cali. She looked up admiringly at Cali as she passed.

Suddenly Cali didn't feel very admirable.

Stacy and Brittan slid over.

"You sit right here," Brittan said, patting the seat by the aisle. Karlyn found room with the two kids on the seat in front of them.

"So Zack found out that Hunter had bet that he would lose the race," Stacy said, starting up with Brittan where she had left off to send Dianne packing.

"Oh, no. What did he say?"

"He swore," Stacy giggled scandalously. "He called him—" Here she put her head closer to Brittan, but spoke loudly enough that Cali could still hear, "a piece of dog poop." Only she used a disgusting word.

Karlyn turned in her seat so she could be a part of the conversation. Something out the back window caught her attention.

"There's your little friend," she said with a grin.

Cali turned around. The back window was grimy. Bus 13 was parked so close that Cali could see everything that was going on. Veronica climbed up the steps and plopped down in the first seat where they had sat together that morning. Leaning into the aisle she asked Mr. Fennelmyer a question. He shook his head and pointed at the bus in front of him. Veronica leaned further out in the aisle and looked. She met Cali's eyes. Disappointment, like the shadow of a cloud on a chilly spring day, swept across Veronica's face.

Rosalie ran up the steps next. She looked out of breath. Cali had the distinct impression that she had been looking for her.

Cali knew she should turn around now. What was coming would not be pleasant. Her stubborn streak didn't allow it. The kids on Bus 13 didn't own her. She would face them without shame.

Veronica said something and pointed. The expression on Rosalie's face made it clear that she didn't want to believe Veronica. Slowly, she turned her head and looked. She met Cali's eyes. There was a moment of disbelief on her face before anger pushed it aside. Her eyes narrowed and her lips tightened.

Cali was afraid. She wasn't there to talk Rosalie down this time. Instead, she was the target. An anger she didn't know she had shoved the fear aside. She had been afraid of Rosalie that morning, but not now.

You just turn me into a frog, she dared, narrowing her own eyes.

For a moment her bravado made her feel tough, invulnerable. Then a voice, her own, sounded in her head.

What, are you stupid?

How tough would she feel when she looked up from the floor through frog eyes while the girls screamed and the boys stomped on her? Would she be able to feel the vibrations and hear the buzzing from here? She expected to see Mr. Fennelmyer grab Rosalie to try to stop her from using her magic. He didn't.

The magic never came. The moment passed and the anger on Rosalie's face evaporated, replaced by a blank look. The look was a thin cover to hide the hurt. The cover was too thin, too delicate, to hide hurt so big. Cali saw it plainly.

"Ow," Cali said, bringing her hand to her heart.

"What?" asked Brittan.

"Ow," Cali said, more loudly this time, grabbing the fabric of her shirt.

"Cali?" inquired Karlyn.

The bus engine roared to life right underneath them. Cali heard the brake release and felt the bus start to roll. She looked directly at Mr. Fennelmyer. His eyes were kind. The expression on his face a mixture of sad happiness, like you feel when a big brother is leaving for college. He gave her a friendly wave that said, "It's been a pleasure to know you."

Who are you? Once more she heard the voice with the sparkles.

"I still don't know," she said, "but I do know I shouldn't be on this bus."

"What?" Stacy and Brittan asked simultaneously.

"Cali, where are you going?" Karlyn called as Cali bolted past. Cali didn't answer.

The first and second buses were rumbling away. Bus 31 slowed for the stop sign at the end of the bus lane. Cali called out, "I'm on the wrong bus."

The bus driver looked into her mirror, surprised. She pressed the brake harder than she meant to. Cali tumbled onto her face next to the bus driver's seat.

"Are you all right?" The driver was startled, angry. "You don't get out of your seat while the bus is moving." She took Cali's hand and helped her to her feet.

"I'm on the wrong bus," Cali said.

"You can't get off now that we're going," said the bus driver.

"Please," Cali said. "I'm on the wrong bus."

"But I stop at your house."

"I know, but I'm still on the wrong bus."

The bus driver's stern look gave way before Cali's pleading eyes. She flicked the switch and the doors opened. Kids stood and leaned into the aisle to see. Eyes followed her as she ran along the bus towards the back. The only eyes she actually saw were Karlyn's. They were sad and hurt.

I'm betraying someone no matter what I do.

Bus 13 had stopped just two feet behind Bus 31. Mr. Fennelmyer had probably slammed on his brakes to avoid a collision. She hoped Marty and Marcus' chemistry set was okay. She stood beside the closed doors. They didn't open. Looking through the window she saw Mr. Fennelmyer gazing down at her, a thoughtful expression on his brow. She felt uneasy. Would he not let her back on?

This decision is not to be made lightly.

She heard his voice even though his mouth didn't move.

Shame filled her as she remembered the flattery she followed onto Bus 31. Perhaps she was no longer worthy of Bus 13. Bus 31 was still there, at the stop sign, waiting for a long line of traffic to pass by. She still had time to go back.

No. She stared up at Mr. Fennelmyer, set her jaw, and knocked on the door—loudly.

His hand moved to the switch. He flicked it and the doors opened. Holding back tears Cali took a big breath, stood up straight, and climbed the steps. She nodded at Mr. Fennelmyer in a dignified manner as she reached the top. Silence and eyes met her as she turned to face the bus.

Veronica looked up at her doubtfully from the front seat. Felicia and Shelley studied her. Jimmy half stood to stare at her. Further back on the other side of the aisle she met Freddy's and Bric's eyes. Standing behind them, Brac gazed at her curiously. In the very back seat three faces topped with raccoon hats rested on hands. They gazed at her suspiciously. Across the aisle Marty and Marcus leaned out to see.

Cali didn't see Rosalie. She had something to say, but she needed to make sure Rosalie was listening. "Where's Rosalie?"

Nobody moved or spoke. They looked at her like she had been accused of something awful. It was unnerving. Finally, from a seat just behind Jimmy, Rosalie's face slowly emerged as she leaned into the aisle. Rosalie had been crying. She didn't look happy to see Cali.

Cali cleared her throat. "I just want you to know that although I'm not particularly peculiar I'm going to be riding this bus, whether you like it or not."

She spoke boldly, showing no fear. Inside she quavered. It mattered to her very much whether they liked it or not. She waited for a sign or a signal that they would accept her odd apology. The silence was agonizing. The weight of their eyes unbearable. Then Jimmy blinked. It was a small thing, but it gave her hope.

Brac broke the silence. "These two doofuses make the supposition that Phineas is more intelligent than Ferb. Clearly the silent Ferb has the intellectual advantage. Where do you stand on this question?"

A smile grew on Cali's face. "What do I think?" Cali said, voice shaking. "I think you're a bunch of dweebs."

"You hear that? She called you two dweebs," Brac said.

"Hear, hear," called out Marty and Marcus from their seat in the back.

"I say the occasion calls for us to whip up some celebratory punch," added Marty.

"All right!" exclaimed Warren. "That stuff gives us the Big Belches."

Cali could hear the clinking of organ pipes being assembled.

"I think a little of Bach's 'The Art of Fugue' would be appropriate right now," Jimmy muttered as he worked.

"You know, if someone would sit down, maybe we could get everyone home on time," said Mr. Fennelmyer, frowning happily

"Sit there," Felicia said, pointing to the seat across the aisle from her and Shelley. "We can talk."

Cali took a step and felt a hand grab hers. Veronica was coming with her. Rosalie stared at Cali morosely. Cali motioned with her hand for Rosalie to come. Rosalie stood slowly and came forward. She pouted all the way. There was just enough room for three of them with Cali in the middle.

Marissa suddenly appeared at their seat. Using her fingers she measured the top of Cali's head.

"We're going to make you a fez for tomorrow," she said. "It's Matt Smith day." Seeing the confused look on Cali's face Marissa rolled her eyes. "You know, *Dr. Who*? He's the 11th Doctor."

"Oh, of course," Cali said. She had heard somewhere that fezzes were cool.

Through all this Cali felt Rosalie staring at her. She looked down into Rosalie's dark eyes. The sadness she saw there moved her.

"I was going to *make* you ride this bus," Rosalie said quietly.

"But you didn't and here I am anyway," Cali said. "How do you suppose that happened?"

Rosalie thought a moment. A small smile formed on her face. It was like a ray of sunshine breaking through storm clouds. "I think it's good magic."

"Magic or not I know it's good to be on Bus 13," Cali said.

Bus 13 travelled up Main Street before turning left on Seventh South. Cali listened to the chatter and the low growl of the engine. The bus was much quieter than it was during the ride to school. She wondered if they'd had all the excitement they were going to have that day.

One of the loudest, most raucous belches Cali had ever heard rang out. It was followed by uncontrolled laughter from the back of the bus.

"Save some for Cali," Brac said. "After all, this is in honor of her."

"Marty, Marcus. How many times have I told you not to start mixing your concoctions until we reach the country?"

"Sorry, Mr. Fennelmyer," both voices called.

"Veronica, your mom and dad are actually going to land when they pick you up this time, right?"

Slow, happy organ tones filled the bus as Jimmy began to play. Shelley was scratching the side of her head just above her ear. Felicia, smiling, stared at Cali. She said nothing, just looked at Cali as if the sight of her made her happy.

A shadow fell over the bus as they left the city limits. An odd thumping and tapping sounded on the roof.

"It's the crows again," Mr. Fennelmyer said. He leaned forward and looked up through the windshield. "Leave the windows up and nobody open the emergency hatch this time."

Butterflies started up in Cali's stomach. "Crows?" she asked.

"Just a bunch of birds," Rosalie said. "What's to be afraid of?"

It was clear to Cali that Rosalie hadn't seen Alfred Hitchcock's movie, *The Birds*. That was probably for the best.

"Birds look at me strange when I'm hanging from my parachute," Veronica said. "Like, 'Who do you think you are?'"

Sing a song of sixpence a pocket full of rye,
Four and twenty blackbirds baked in a pie:

It was Bric, Brac, and Freddy, singing the first lines of a nursery rhyme Cali had heard before.

What a strange bus, she thought.

The tapping on the roof grew louder and she heard the beating of wings.

"Marty, Marcus, we might need some of your crow repellent," yelled Mr. Fennelmyer.

There was a long belch, and then, "We're on it."

Cali felt a hand slip into hers. She looked down into Rosalie's smiling face.

Yes, a strange bus and I'm part of it.

Amid the organ music, the belching, the nursery rhyme, and the tapping, Cali realized that she felt at home.

ABOUT THE AUTHOR

Before he gave up on being practical and normal Tory spent fifteen years in the high tech industry traveling the world. During these years he and his wife, Barbara, had eight children. Tory could often be seen busing his family around in a tan minivan. Driving a school bus was the next, inevitable step. Of course, the final destination was always writing. In addition to *The Peculiar Children of Bus 13*, Tory has written *Joey and the Magic Map* and *Jacob and Lace*. If you like the books Tory writes feel free to leave a book review on Amazon.com and Goodreads.com. Tory currently lives with his wife and children in Levan, Utah, a lovely spot where you can still see the Milky Way.

Other Book By Tory Anderson —Available on Amazon

In a new town, a new school, and with a mother losing her battle with depression, Jacob's life is turned upside-down. Lace Pearlshom, the social outcast from Jacob's homeroom, adds to the confusion with her uncanny way of appearing out of shadows and disappearing up blind alleys. She pushes her way, unwelcome, into Jacob's life. Lace may hold the key to saving Jacob's mother, but can he accept the cost?

Joey Johanaby thought his life ended when his dad died. Being forced to move with into a mysterious, old, Southern mansion in Tennessee seems to make things worse. The mansion is home to more than Joey and his family. Ghostly and magical characters from the mansion's past take an interest in Joey and his struggles. They want to help, but their quirky methods are questionable. After the family is almost torn apart by a near-tragedy Joey obtains a magic map. With this map Joey goes on a journey that he might not return from—a journey that changes him forever.

CPSIA information can be obtained
at www.ICGtesting.com
Printed in the USA
LVHW041016040819
626455LV00017B/817